TRUTH

ABOUT

US

B. CELESTE

THE TRUTH ABOUT US

Ollie and Charlie against the world.

B. CELESTE

Playlist

"I Don't Want to Miss a Thing" – Aerosmith
"Perfect" – Ed Sheeran
"Lover" – Taylor Swift
"From the Ground Up" – Dan + Shay
"Team" – Noah Cyrus & Max
"A Thousand Years" – Christina Perri
"You Are the Reason" – Calum Scott
"Amazed" – Lonestar
"You and Me" – Lifehouse
"Speechless" – Dan + Shay

To everyone who loved Charlie and Ollie –
This is for you

PROLOGUE

Charlie / 25

A single sound can tilt the axis your entire world rests on in a second flat. That same sound drowns out all the others surrounding you—the mechanical beeping of new-age technology, the nurses shuffling around the room, and the doctor speaking his congratulations at the tiny squirming bundle in his arms.

Then reality takes over, and you realize there's nothing you can do to protect them from the world you've brought them into. First-hand experience tells me anything can happen the moment you take your first breath. Deep down, as the beautiful baby boy is set in my waiting arms, I know I would give my life for him.

My husband leans forward, letting a tear drop from the tip of his nose down to the newborn's head. "He's beautiful, Charlie. He's..." Oliver James chokes on emotion, gripping my arm and shaking his head as he examines the warm-blooded creation mixed of our DNA that shouldn't morally exist if we'd followed the rules.

I stare so intently, yet so absently, at the being I've loved so wholeheartedly for just over nine months. He moves and makes the softest wail that sounds nothing like I've ever heard.

And I know.

I know that everything has changed.

One of the white-haired nurses walks over and smiles at the sight of us. "We need to clean him and take him for some basic tests."

Instantly, my heart thunders and arms cradle him closer to my bare breasts. Ollie's hand caresses the back of Milo's head before leaning forward and pressing a kiss to the side of my sweaty temple.

"We'll bring him right back," the nurse promises, her eyes kind but not fully trustworthy. Her position should have told me to just loosen my grip and let them do what they needed.

It's Ollie's reassurance that has me slowly nodding and exhaling a pained breath. "I know, Charlie. But they need to do their job."

Swallowing is nearly impossible as I manage to let the nurse take him from me. Her lean figure becomes blurry as I stare at the two of them, my chest rising and falling heavily while Ollie coaxes me into trying to take a deep breath.

"Milo." My voice cracks as my hand flies to my husband's arm. "You need to go with him, Ollie. Please? I can't protect him."

The heart monitor goes off in rapid commotion, causing one of the other nurses to turn her focus on me. Ollie's conflicted gaze darts between me and our son, worry etched into his features that pull him in both directions.

"Please," I beg, letting tears fall from emotion I can't control. There's a gaping hole in my heart that appeared as soon as I delivered the final push. I feel too much. I feel nothing. There's no balance between the two extremes.

"Honey, I need you to try calming down," the dark-skinned nurse instructs, gently placing her hand on mine. "Milo is going to be just fine."

My eyes stray to Ollie's before mouthing, *please?* The last time I begged so brokenly was under far darker circumstances. My mind locked away those memories behind cast iron bars that took years of therapy to find a key to. The feeling is so similar, so heavy and raw on the soul I no longer feel as though I carry fully. Part of it is in the flesh with dark eyes staring back at me.

Ollie dips down again and lingers a kiss on the top of my head, giving my hand a squeeze. He follows the nurse carrying Milo out, leaving me hyperventilating on the bed of damp and bloody sheets until the machines ring noisily around me.

"Charlie," the doctor instructs, coming into the hazy view of my vision. His dark hair is peppered with gray and white and the wrinkles by his aged eyes become more predominate as concern washes over his face. "Can you hear me, Charlie?"

A hand touches mine, then another reaches for my face. People talk and call my name, but I don't fully hear them past the racing of my heart and the ringing in my ears. I want Milo and Ollie and a sense of peace that seem so far out of reach.

"She's in shock," someone states from close by, causing rushed murmurs around the room of staff still littering the small area.

Is that what I am? Shocked. Subconsciously, there's a maternal need to get out of bed and hunt down my son. The physical and mental opposition to that keeps me planted in bed, dazed from the people around me.

I blink and the doctor is there.

I blink again and the nurses are there.

But Milo isn't. My sweet, innocent Milo is in a world that is full of corruption I know all too well. Despite the firm belief that Ollie will be the perfect father, better than one could ever truly want, it doesn't stop my mind from swelling with the unknown *what ifs* thrown into the mixture.

It's a gut feeling that something is wrong, like his reactions to people weren't quite right. Perhaps if the nurse hadn't shared a microscopic look with the doctor as if they saw the same thing, I wouldn't race to a conclusion nobody but they would know with time.

The feeling remains. My body aches with awareness and pain and something so deeply woven into my bones that I fear I'm broken far worse than I was by my past.

I love Milo, that much I know.

But there's another overwhelming feeling that detaches me from the other swirling emotions trying to fill the hole in my chest. As though the cement is the concern rather than the pure love that I know is stitching together the wound caused by something beyond me. Something I want to go away.

I acknowledge that something is wrong with the way my mind and heart react to the very moment in my life I've both been dreading and looking forward to for the past few months. My senses become hyperaware of the people asking me questions and the machines easing their high-pitched reactions to my resting body. Dr. Rosehill praises me and pats my hand, and the nurses share a look of relief as they continue cleaning the room and telling me the next steps.

I count the minutes that drag on, my eyes never straying from the open door to the right, waiting for the moment I see a blue blanket wrapped around the boy I've been dying to meet for far too long. What I don't expect is the presence of an empty-handed man who put a second ring on my finger in an intimate ceremony just months after asking me to marry him.

"He's getting more tests done," he assures as soon as he meets my bleak eyes. The way he kneels by my bed and takes my hand confirms what I've suspected. But it's the way he smiles as if everything is okay that sets me off, because I know what Ollie looks like when he's happy, in love, or any array of emotions that offers a genuine quirk to his lips.

This one is distant and pained and worried. A look he gave me when we visited Bridgeport, and everyone stared at our hands clasped in one another's. The fourteen-year age difference seems like nothing compared to the weight dawning his chocolate eyes.

"Oliver," I whisper, swallowing what feels like rusty nails and dirty water.

Her fingers weave in mine. "Milo is healthy, Charlie. He's healthy and he's going to be okay. But..."

I blink.

I wait.

I hold my breath.

"He failed his hearing test, baby."

Staring at him like I don't understand, my lips part with an uneven exhale. But the signs build in the back of my consciousness that tell me *I told you so*—the anxiety-ridden moments that perhaps something was wrong when I'd play the piano or sing and feel no movement in response. It left us with piles of bills from emergency room visits for ultrasounds and explanations. Then I'd hear a heartbeat and feel the tiniest little kick and know that everything is okay.

"But he's healthy," he repeats, nodding encouragingly as I wrap my head around the news. Ollie is good like that. He gives me time and space, but not too much of either. We've always functioned better as a team. Ollie and Charlie against the world. And too often, it felt just like that.

Because the world is a cruel place with judgements thrown over the unconventional dynamics between our circumstances. How we met and how we loved and how easily it was too fall into the forbidden.

Our love is unforgiving though.

Just like it is with Milo.

"He's healthy," I say slowly, finding my voice and tightening my hold on him. "He's really okay, Ollie?"

Ollie's brown eyes glaze with oncoming tears that don't make it past his thick lashes. "Our son is more than that, Charlie. He's fucking perfect. God, he's everything and more."

And the tears that I've saved for this very moment spill from my own eyes and drown my flushed cheeks. The months of discomfort, hours of pushing, and pain I've already forgotten about were all worth the news delivered to me.

We hold each other and cry and smile and breathe a sigh of relief that we've welcomed something so pure into the world we've created for ourselves despite the whispers and stares.

Milo Brahm James.

One Year Later

ONE

Ollie

The smooth melody of caressed ivory slows with each note nearing its end as I quietly close the door. I hear the piano first, then the sultry voice accompanying the tune of a soft sung lullaby. A smile can't help but form at the corners of my lips as I make my way down the hall to our makeshift music room that Charlie has music therapy lessons in.

Pressing my back against the wall just outside the open door, I close my eyes and listen to Charlie sing to our son. I know he's watching her in fascination and love, with a dopey look on his mesmerized face. They do this every day like clockwork. Charlie never lets Milo's condition waver her determination to introduce music into his life.

Music therapy is her passion outside of motherhood, and she's blended the two in a song of its own at home. When I watch them after work every night, I notice how Milo's tiny hands press against the piano just like Charlie taught him to. I mimicked him once, feeling the vibration of each note ricochet through my body like a silent song.

"I know you're out there," she accuses. The music stops abruptly. I round the corner and smile at her waiting form on the bench—her blonde hair in a messy bun and her face without a stitch of makeup.

Kissing her lips, I bend down and pick up Milo. The grin on his chubby face as he palms my cheeks fills my chest with the purest level of happiness I've ever had the pleasure of experiencing. "Hey, buddy. Have a good day with Mommy?"

Charlie swings her legs to the opposite side of the bench and watches us. "We saw River today. She brought Lucas and Maddie with her for a playdate."

My lips twitch upward at the news of my sister's visit. Her first biological kid, Luke, is great with Milo. But Maddie doesn't understand that he can't hear her and takes it personally when he doesn't react. The difference in patience between them always makes me nervous when I see Maddie throw a fit and Milo stare absently wondering what he did wrong.

Milo blows drool-ridden bubbles at me as I bounce him in my arms, making me chuckle and kiss his cheek until his hands grab a fistful of my hair and yanks. Wincing at the pain, I detach his oddly strong hold and wiggle his hand at Charlie. Her gem-like green eyes are bright as she watches us contently, her elbow resting on the covered piano keys behind her.

She reaches up and tickles Milo's socked feet, making

him smile and squirm at her until his arms stretch in her direction. As I deposit him in her waiting arms, I ask, "How are River and the kids doing?"

Milo latches onto the collar of Charlie's shirt, pulling it so the peaks of her perky breasts tease my vision. She lets him play, bouncing her knees as she focuses on me. "Luke advanced another reading level in school. River thinks if he keeps it up, he may skip a grade when he's older. Maddie lost her first tooth and tried convincing Everett that the tooth fairy gives kids five dollars a tooth now."

I laugh, shaking my head at the tenacious five-year-old's logic. Maddie has never wanted anything less than what she thinks she deserves. I remember River admitting how bad the terrible twos were, which then extended into the threes. The word "no" is Maddie's least favorite to hear, and she made it known whenever it was spoken. It doesn't help that she's got Everett wrapped around her finger. He tries playing the bad guy, but all it takes is Maddie looking up with those mint puppy dog eyes before he's gone.

I bet she'll get ten dollars from him.

"You'd be no different," she insists, standing with Milo perched on her side. We walk out of the music room and into the kitchen, where I grab a bottle from the fridge and prepare it for Milo while Charlie takes a seat at the table.

"I'm not denying it." Once I'm done, I walk over and pass her the bottle to give to him. He takes it greedily, latching on with both his hands and glancing back at both of us.

The blond hair he gets from Charlie has gotten thicker. His first haircut was a couple months ago, and Charlie teared up when the first strand hit the floor. I collected a chunk and saved it for the scrapbook she started, which is already half full of memorabilia and photographs from the past fourteen months.

Clearing my throat, I walk back around the island and busy myself with getting dinner ready. "And Everett? Did she mention how he's been doing?"

Everett Tucker, my oldest childhood friend, and I have our issues. I've taken responsibility for my contribution from the tension that's still buried under certain topics, but we've worked past most of the problems as the years pass. He'll never fully forgive me for going after Charlie when she was underage, but on the off days he's reminded of our fourteen-year age difference, he doesn't bring it up. It doesn't stop the familiar darkening of his eyes when he watches Charlie and I interact—especially with Milo in the picture.

Charlie understands my hesitation in bringing him up. We've both experienced ups and downs since choosing to make our relationship work. She loves Everett and River and wants their approval and love no matter what. I can tell the rift between Rhett and I bothers her, but it's nowhere near as tense as it used to be. All of us have conversations like adults catching up, and most of the time there's no awkwardness. But there's always a reminder of the choices we made that brings back the thick silence of a conversation everyone does their best to avoid, especially when my parents are involved.

Bridgette and Robert James, though skeptical and disapproving of my decision to pursue Charlie, support our relationship. Maybe if it wasn't really love they would have both tried harder to get me to see reason. But reason was out the door with Charlie from the start. It didn't matter that Everett and River brought her into my life, she felt like mine from the start.

My friend.

My family.

More.

"He's been busy, as you can imagine." A hint of humor sparks in her eyes. She finds my discomfort over asking about him amusing. I'm not sure she'll ever fully understand my caution, but at least I can be entertaining. "There are other rival companies trying to get a buy-in that's been cutting into his business, so he's been stressed trying to balance everything. River didn't say it outright, but I think it may be good if him and you did something together to get his mind off things. You know, like a bro date."

I blink. "A bro date," I repeat.

She simply nods, setting the bottle down on the table once Milo is finished and patting his back as he reaches for a loose piece of her hair that's fallen from her updo. "Yeah, like a guy day. Maybe you guys can go grab a drink or, I don't know, play basketball. You never do that anymore."

I don't know if she means I don't hang out with him like we used to or play ball like we found time to do in the past. Either way, we're older now and have families to take care of. "Why don't we invite them over for dinner this weekend? The game is Sunday. You and River can gossip about whatever the hell you talk about, and Rhett and I can watch the game after we eat."

She contemplates the answer, seemingly liking the idea. "Fine. You're calling and inviting them though. River said she hasn't heard from you in a week and I'm sure Everett wouldn't mind catching up."

Part of me feels like I owe him for the stress taking over my father's company has plagued him with. If I'd followed in Robert James' footsteps, I'd be the one wearing a suit and tie and worrying about shit like budget mods and business rivalries.

Milo wiggles in Charlie's lap until she lets him down. He crawls over to me, plopping down on his butt, and plays with my pantleg.

I kneel. "What's up, bud?"

He just stares at me.

I bring up the topic that I've been nervous to speak of since it was suggested. Running my hand through his hair, I say, "We still have the option to look into the cochlear implants. He's getting older—"

"No."

Sighing, I look up at her. "I get why you said no after

he was born, but he's over one now, babe. There's limited risk and far more benefits. We have the money."

Charlie's eyes dip to our son, who has occupied himself with his own toes. "He's too young to understand what it takes to have those. I want what's best for him too, Ollie, but I still think we should wait."

"I know you're scared," I offer softly, "but we'll get the best doctors. Imagine what his reaction would be when he hears for the first time. Technology can do that nowadays."

She stands, shaking her head. "I love you, but I'm saying no. He's been doing just fine so far without the surgery. We can discuss it when he's older."

As she tries leaving, I gently wrap my palm around her arm and draw her to me. My hand falls from her bicep and onto her hip, my eyes meeting hers. "He should get them before he starts school. Think about it, Charlie. Do we want him to miss school after he starts for the procedure? He'll need time to adjust."

I know her worry. She's been doing everything in her power to make sure he's protected. In her sleep, she'll say his name in the softest plea, like she's praying for his safety, and it kills me a little inside. She's afraid something will happen that she can't control. Given her history, it's understandable. But the longer we wait to go through with the implants, the harder it may be for him to cope with the change.

My other hand hooks around her waist, pulling her closer so she's pressed against my front. "We both love him and want what's best. I think we need to sit down and talk about it."

When she doesn't say anything, I take it as a small victory. Her eyes go from me to Milo, her front teeth biting down onto her bottom lip. It tells me she knows I'm right, but there's a fear I'll never fully grasp. She carried him for nine months, cared for him in such an intimate way, and now has to make a big decision.

"You don't have to do it alone," I remind her, brushing my lips against hers. Lingering over the plush mouth I've gotten to know well, I nuzzle my nose against hers. "You never have to do it alone, okay?"

Slowly, she nods. Kissing me again, she whispers, "I love you, Oliver James."

There aren't words that can describe what I feel for her—the mother of my child, the woman built for me.

But I settle with, "I love you too, baby."

TWO

Charlie

Gentle kisses trail down the back of my neck and bare shoulders, stopping at the edge of the oversized tee I wear. A warm hand glides over my hip, curving until fingertips dig into my flesh. I keep hold of the tablet I'm reading on, ignoring the advances that leave goosebumps over my arms and continue scanning the words across the screen instead.

"You've been reading for hours," Ollie whispers, moving the shirt further down my arm to expose more skin. "It won't go anywhere. You can look over the information tomorrow."

Letting it lower slightly, I turn my head over my shoulder and meet soft lips. He lets the kiss linger for a moment before pulling back. "I know," I relent, "but the doctor gave us so much to look at. I feel like I need to be prepared."

Ollie sits up and glances at the tablet screen, letting his dark eyes trail over the words before meeting mine again. "He told you not to look up anything online. You're going to make yourself sick from stress."

"Did you know that the hearing device implements sounds through a processer? It uses electrodes, Ollie. Like ... electricity or something. That's scary. Do we want electricity going anywhere near our baby's head?"

"Babe, I doubt it's as bad as the internet makes it out to be. These procedures are more common nowadays with great success rates. Don't forget that tidbit we were told."

"But, Oll—"

He peels the tablet from me, powering it off and setting it on his nightstand. "I'm not letting you do this to yourself. Dr. Woodshed gave us plenty of legitimate sources so we can make our final decision."

Ollie hooks an arm around my waist and pulls me into his solid front. "The audiologist knows what he's talking about, Charlie. We made sure we found the one with the best reputation. We need to trust him."

"The surgery—"

"Will be worth it," he insists, kissing my cheek. I turn around so we're facing each other, my head resting on his chest as he drapes an arm over my shoulder.

"I know." I wet my bottom lip. "He's the sweetest little boy, Ollie. What if something bad happens and he's never the same?"

His hold on me tightens. "He won't be. Isn't that the point? Milo is stubborn, just like someone else I know."

Tipping my chin up, I meet his eyes. "I knew nothing bad would happen to him during the pregnancy. Every choice I made was for him and his health. And when you told me ... when I found out he was deaf, I wondered what I did wrong. Did I eat something bad? Not rest enough? All I wanted was to be sure nobody could harm him. So why does it feel like I failed?"

His eyes soften. "You did nothing wrong, Charlie. Do you hear me? The doctors all said that you did everything as you should have during the pregnancy. The genes just didn't line up in his favor. Sometimes things happen, and I know you don't like hearing that but it's true. Milo is still a healthy baby. His impairment just makes him stronger. Just like his mother."

I bite down on my inner cheek, not knowing what to say. Doubt creeps into my conscious the longer I think about it. How many times had I planned on teaching him music? The piano? I spoke to my unborn baby about my plans for his future, and he couldn't hear a word.

When the doctors explained that Milo got mutated recessive genes from both Ollie and I that caused the hair in his middle ear not to form, I was speechless. It took a while to grasp that those hairs are what transmit sound waves to the brain. The lack of something so little caused something so big. Realistically, there is nothing that could have prevented it from happening. I know it isn't directly my fault.

Tears well in my eyes. "He doesn't know what I sound like."

Ollie pulls me on top of him, hugging me close. My tears soak into the crook of his neck. He rubs circles over my back and hushes me in comfort. "He doesn't need to hear your voice to love you unconditionally. You're his entire world, baby."

I know it's true, but there are too many emotions to sort through to see logic. Ollie just keeps holding me until the tears subside. His hands rub my back, comb through my messy hair, and give me warmth when I feel the cool depths of maternal guilt freeze me from the inside out.

When I collect myself, all I can think about is the heat from his body—how bad I need it to thaw my cold limbs. He gives me everything I need without hesitation, meeting my lips halfway and letting me part his and swipe his tongue. My legs straddle his, my hands trailing between us and grabbing at the hem of his shirt, before he helps me strip it off him. He tastes like the mint from our toothpaste, cold and inviting in an entirely new way. My palms drag down his bare chest, still sculpted from all the time he spends working out in our little home gym. The images of him playing with Milo on the blue mats he bought for our son to tumble around on has my mouth demanding more.

Each stroke of his tongue sends me in a frenzy that sheds more of our clothes. His sweatpants, my tee, his boxers, and my thong. Before I know it, our hands are exploring each other's bodies in a desperate plea that sings to my heart. His fingers find my soaked entrance, working my slit from bottom to top and playing with the bundle of nerves that has my body sparking with need.

My palm grips him and jerks up and down in an uneven pace until he's steel in my hold.

"Fuck, baby," he groans, twitching and moving two fingers inside of me. "Always so fucking good with you."

I grind against his fingers, silently begging for more friction. "Do you remember what it was like the first time? How you fought so hard because you knew it was wrong but couldn't stop? I've always loved how you feel inside me. But then? You changed everything."

He grips my hair and yanks me into him, kissing me fiercely and unapologetically. My orgasm builds fast when he picks up the pace and dominates my mouth. The grip I have on his rock-hard cock loosens when I begin quaking around him, moaning into his mouth and riding out the sensations he brings me.

Lifting up the same time he guides himself to my entrance, I slide down until he's hilt deep inside of me. My palms grip his shoulders and I move, rocking over him and grinding down until his hands go to my hips. He digs his nails into me, picking me up and meeting my hips thrust for thrust.

"I replay our first time all the time," he tells me with heated eyes. "I fucking hated myself for giving in when you climbed on top of me that day. But no matter how many times I tell myself it shouldn't have happened, I'm glad it did. I wanted you before I should have and will keep you for life. You're *mine*, Charlie."

My head tips back as he holds my hips down and fucks me from below. His pelvic bone rubs against my clit in such a delicious way that my vision dots and my lips part with heavy pants.

"Yours," I promise, listening to the sound of our bodies coming together. The heat building in my limbs sets me on fire, and nothing can douse the flames. No longer am I cold from guilt, but in love—so in love with this man and the life we've built together.

He flips us over so quickly that I yelp, then moan as he positions my legs over his shoulders and thrusts back into me. His cock works me from this new position and leaves me incoherent and writhing. I grab fistfuls of the sheets as my body moves up the bed. He holds my head to protect it from hitting the wooden headboard that smacks the wall with every move.

"Never going to get tired of this," he says, sweat covering his chest. "You're it for me, Charlie. Always."

Nodding along to everything he says, I pant, "Today. Tomorrow. Always. Always, Oliver James. I love you so fucking much."

It hurts to be so consumed by someone, but this pain is tolerable and welcome in a world full of far darker things. The feeling in my chest that suffocates me is because I'm happily tortured. My problems are nothing compared to what they used to be, and I have two beautiful individuals in my life that have my back no matter what.

Ollie bends my leg forward, deepening his thrusts until I claw at his chest and come hard. He jackknifes into me a few more times before I feel him fill me.

Dampness runs down my leg as he pulls out, dropping onto his side and pulling me into him again.

He pecks my cheek. "Let's take the weekend off from worrying about doctor appointments. Everett and River will be here Sunday. That'll help take our minds off it a little."

I find myself nodding, finding his hand and weaving my fingers into his. "What do you think his reaction will be when he hears for the first time?"

He squeezes my hand. "He'll look at you with wide eyes and smile because he just heard the most beautiful person speaking to him."

My heart flutters. Nuzzling into his side, I let the silence fill the tiny crevices doubt creeps into. Ollie is right like he usually is, but that doesn't make it easier to swallow.

"Stop thinking," he whispers.

If only it were that easy.

THREE

Ollie

The sound of tires slowing outside the front door has Charlie squeezing my hand tightly before giving me a reassuring smile. Our son coos in her hold, reaching out to me and flexing his hands for me to take him.

"I'll get the food out," she says, passing Milo over and pecking my cheek before kissing his temple. "Remember. Bro date."

Rolling my eyes, I swat her ass and walk to the door right as the bell rings. Milo drools on my arm, then wipes his mouth on my shirt before squirming at the sight of River as soon as the door opens. Her bright smile mirrors the one on both Milo's and I's faces.

"Ollie," she greets, giving me a side hug while Luke and Maddie enter beside me. My sister's dark eyes light up as they connect with Milo, lifting them in question.

Chuckling, I pass him to her and watch as she pinches his cheeks and plants kisses all over his face. "He looks more and more like you every time I see him. I swear it."

A car door closes and footsteps near until Everett

appears behind River. He notes Milo already wrapped in her arms and smiles with a shake of his head. He guides River further in so he can close the front door, turning to me with a tip to his head as greeting.

"Oliver." We shake hands and smile at one another. It's no different than any other time. If anything, it's more mature than the half ass shake-turned-hug we'd do when we were younger. To think we're both going to be forty soon still escapes me because it feels like just yesterday we were playing basketball for the Bridgeport Patriots team.

We all walk into the kitchen side by side, River focusing on Milo more than her husband or me. Luke and Maddie are on either side of Charlie as she sets the meat to be grilled down on the counter.

"Need help?" Rhett asks, gesturing toward the hamburger patties Charlie and I made this morning.

I notice the way Charlie's lips tilt like she's prodding me to say yes. She does everything in her power to make sure Rhett and I get along, and River finds it just as amusing as I do even though there's nothing to worry about.

"Sure." We grab some of the food and head out the back door attached to the kitchen. Our backyard has plenty of room for the kids to play, a little swing set and slide that Dad helped me put together, and a fire pit and grill off to the side. Once in a while we'll have little summer barbecues and light a fire to make s'mores, which started last year during July fourth when Maddie admitted she'd never had them before. Now she begs us to break out marshmallows every time they visit. If anything, her sugar addiction is the reason Everett would hate me now.

"River mentioned work has been rough." I cleaned the grill off earlier, so I spray the metal racks and fire it up. Looking up at him with one hand in his blue jeans, I ask, "Anything I could help with?"

My degree in business was a waste of money and time, and something Dad still brings up when I complain about my salary at the school I coach at. Granted, it would make more sense to find something that pays better using the piece of paper I acquired after years of schooling at Penn State, but it isn't what I want to do. Robert James doesn't usually push when I remind him of that, but I can tell disappointment lingers after the conversation is over.

"Nah, man. I'll handle it."

His tired features age his face with the slightest marks around his eyes. The darker bags contrast the abnormal mint eyes that he passed along to both Luke and Maddie, making me wonder when the last time he's gotten a full night's sleep was.

When the grill is hot enough, I set the burgers on it, lining them up and leaving room for the chicken breasts Charlie marinated in barbecue sauce as a different option. Luke is already a bottomless pit that makes me nervous for Milo to get older, and Maddie is pickier than any child I've ever known. Charlie got up early this morning to prepare a regular salad, potato salad, and even macaroni and cheese hoping the kids would find something they liked to eat.

Everett clears his throat, eyeing the window that shows River and Charlie laughing over something Milo does. "How's everything been? River told me the other night that you and Charlie went to see a specialist for Milo."

Watching Charlie play with Milo makes my body ease as I grab the metal tongs and start placing the chicken on the rack. The sizzling of the sauce fills the minor silence between us as I gather my thoughts.

"She's scared," I tell him quietly, eyeing the women in the house. "Milo doesn't let his condition stop him from being happy, you know? I think on top of worrying about the surgery, she thinks that he won't be able to adjust. It's for life, Rhett. That's ... shit, it's terrifying."

His hand comes down on my shoulder, giving it one quick squeeze before dropping it back to his side. "I know things with us haven't been easy, but if you ever need help with anything..."

Giving him a grateful smile, I turn my focus downward on the food. "I appreciate it, but there's nothing you can help us with right now. We see the doctor again next week to go over the next steps—insurance, another hearing test, figuring out what device would work best, and there's way more following the surgery." My throat tightens as I force a breath. "I get why she's hesitant. He's too young to understand what's going on and he can't make this decision on his own. That's huge for her."

He nods sympathetically. "It would be for any parent, Ollie."

It's different for Charlie though, and he doesn't fully grasp that. Her choices were taken away from her growing up, long before River and Everett took her out of foster care and adopted her into their family. She wants to keep control in her life and never put her children through what she did. It's admirable.

Trying to clear the lump building in my throat, I flip a few of the patties. "We have to make this life changing decision for Milo, and we're both worried it's not the best one. The shit people say to us makes us think that we could mess him up by trying to give him the ability to hear. Then we fail as parents."

"Stop." His voice is hard as he takes the spatula from me and moves me away from the grill so he can take over. "I may struggle with understanding your relationship with Charlie given the circumstances, but you want to know why I accept it? Why I don't want to throw another punch like the day I found out about you two?"

My jaw moves but I say nothing.

"You love each other." He flips the meat and glances at me. One of his hands gestures towards the house, his finger shaking at the window. "More importantly, you love that little boy in there. Whatever choice you two make for Milo doesn't make you bad parents. If anything, you're a better one for weighing those options. And you know what? Fuck everyone else. All you need to listen to is Charlie and the doctors who specialize in this. You and I both know that everybody else's opinions don't matter."

He's got me there. His rocky start to the relationship with River earned him a lot of backlash back home. That's no different than me and Charlie knowing how old she was when we started getting involved—not to mention who she is to me. One thing all of us learned over the years is that love that's meant to last survives the trials. We still get looks from time to time when we visit my parents and show up at our go-to café hand in hand. It used to make me uncomfortable, like any minute I was about to be arrested and shoved into the back of a police car for the choices we made too soon regarding our relationship.

But here we are.

Married. One kid. In love.

I find myself saying, "You're right."

Before our conversation continues, the door opens, and Luke walks out with two bottles of beer in his hand. He walks over to Everett first, handing his father one before holding out the second to me. "Mom told me to bring you guys drinks. I think they just wanted me to make sure you weren't fighting or something."

My brows arch and Rhett just snickers, messing up Lucas's brown hair. In the sunlight there are dirty blond highlights he gets from Everett, but the hair and light skin tone are all River. Maddie is the same. It makes me wonder if Milo will somehow grow to look more like one of us instead of a perfect mixture like he is now.

"We're fine, kid," I note, opening the beer and shaking my head with an amused smile on my face. "Want to help us out? There should be a serving platter in the kitchen. Charlie will show you where. Mind bringing it out so I can get the chicken on it?"

He just nods and walks back in.

I turn to Everett with a quirked brow. "I know River has mentioned he's smart, but the kid is perceptive as hell."

Rhett nods, his grin disappearing as he glances quickly at the house before turning back to me. "Sometimes I worry about him. I think kids have brought some shit up to him about..." He tips his chin at me. "You know, just stuff they've probably heard their parents say. But he's observant. He knows that our family dynamics are ... unusual."

I curse. "He's getting bullied over it?"

His tongue clicks with a loose shrug, trying to keep things casual. "That and being above his classmates in just about every subject. Kids think he's weird. I overheard him talk to River about it the other day. He's having trouble fitting in because of everything."

I rub the back of my neck. "Is he okay?"

The door opens again, and Luke comes out holding a plate in his hands. I take it with a smile and notice the dullness to his eyes. Nudging him with my arm, I set the plate down on the shelf attached to the grill. "Do you want to watch the game with us after we eat? I hear you're into sports."

Luke kicks at the grass, lifting his shoulders and dropping them. "I was thinking maybe Maddie and I can hang out with Charlie. She said she'd teach us more notes on the piano."

That lifts my lips. "That sounds like a great plan, bud. She's been telling me how quickly you've picked it up."

Luke chances a glance at me, thick lashes framing his green eyes. "Maddie's upset because she's not learning as fast. I'm trying to help her, but she won't listen."

Everett takes over. "Your sister is stubborn. She just needs to focus, but maybe music isn't her thing. I think she just likes hanging out with you."

Those two are close. Charlie told me once that they reminded her of me and River. Luke looks out for Maddie and Maddie looks up to him. They rarely bicker and seem to get along most of the time, more friends than siblings.

I can tell he likes the idea of Maddie learning piano for him. He doesn't let his lips waver for very long, letting the drop into a neutral position. "When's lunch? I'm hungry."

Everett and I laugh. Rhett says, "About ten minutes. Why don't you go help the girls set the table? We'll be in shortly."

"There are a few different salads in the fridge," I chime in when he's at the door. "If you can get those out, I'd appreciate it."

When he disappears, I just listen to the distant noise inside and shake my head. "It's crazy."

He turns to me.

"We have families."

He grunts. "We're getting old."

Snickering, I hold the plate up for him to start depositing the cooked meat on. "Some of us are aging better than others."

His glare is mixed with amusement. "I bet you'd be graying too if you decided to run a multi-million-dollar company, Pretty Boy." His grin reappears. "But at least I have the brains."

"Burn." I laugh and nudge his shoulder.

As we walk toward the house, he slows his steps. "Everything is going to be okay, Ollie. Milo, Charlie, Luke, all of us will be fine."

And I believe him.

FOUR

Charlie

Humming along to the song as each key is pressed by my fingers, I close my eyes and absorb what would be the sound of high-pitched notes filling the otherwise quiet room. My fingers drift along the ivory, focusing on three different notes as I rock my head to the beat.

The vibrations travel up my arm, leaving me focused on the sensation rather than the other senses I'm used to narrowing in on. Fumbling over the keys for a few seconds, my chest clogs with emotion knowing this is what Milo hears.

Nothing.

Yelping when the noise canceling headphones are taken off me, I whip around and see Ollie standing there with Milo in his arms. His eyes are sad, knowing, as he carefully sets the headphones down on the bench beside me.

"I was just practicing," I murmur.

He bends down and kisses me. "I know."

Closing the key lid, I stand up and tickle Milo's tummy. A huge smile spreads across his face as he wiggles in Ollie's hold. Instead of reaching for me, he grabs onto Ollie's sweatshirt and makes drool bubbles at me.

Giggling, I kiss his cheek. "You're so silly, baby boy." My eyes meet my husband's as our hands find each other's. "Get all your errands run?"

He tugs my hand, weaving our fingers together and guiding me out of the room. "We did. How about we go to the park for a little while? The weather is perfect out."

"Can we go out for dinner after?"

His smirk is devious. "Does that mean actual dinner or donuts again?"

I shove his shoulder playfully and grab the stroller from the closet by the door. "I'm always down for both. But I was thinking Chinese. Or the new Indian place."

The face he makes says Indian is out. "I thought you hated Indian food. You said it gave you heartburn."

"Sometimes it's worth it."

He snickers and gets Milo stationed in the stroller before standing and stopping me from closing the door completely. Brows pinched in confusion, I watch as he walks into the closet and shuffles around for something.

I groan when he steps out, producing a familiar pink skateboard in his hands. "No. Ollie, I haven't done that in forever."

He passes it to me. "Exactly. Live a little, Charlie. We'll go out and enjoy the sunshine, and you can remind me what a badass you are."

My eyes roll as I slide the board under my arm. "I

don't think skateboarding makes me very badass, but whatever."

"Do it for Milo."

That's not playing fair. He knows I'd do anything for the chubby little baby that's currently chewing on his fingers and blinking up at me from where he's sitting. "Fine, but you're getting on this too."

"I don't think—"

I open the door and glance at him over my shoulder. "What, old man? Afraid you'll throw out your back? Live a little."

He levels with me with an amused expression painting his features. "Always a smartass, huh?"

I stick my tongue out. "Yet you love me."

"Always."

I NEVER THOUGHT I'D SEE OLLIE LOOK SO PALE OVER something as mundane as skateboarding, but the shade of his skin as he tries balancing on the bright pink board under his feet shows his nerves. With one hand on Milo's stroller and the other helping him get stable, I direct him on what to do just like Liam did with me when I was learning how to board in Chicago.

"Breathe." I try hiding my wavering lips, but I can't help it. "Ollie, just breathe. You look like you want to hurl. That'd be embarrassing."

He eyes me. "More embarrassing than wiping out flat on my face in front of our son?"

I weigh the options in contemplation before shrugging. "Everyone wipes out. Remember when I got hurt and you almost ripped Liam's hands off when you saw him carrying me on his back afterwards? You know, before you ditched me and our movie night."

He seemingly forgets his current predicament and stares at me unblinking. "How do you even remember that?"

How could I forget watching him walk away from me? I know what he did to try forgetting me. I smelled the perfume lingering in his apartment whenever we'd get into a fight. To think he was probably ditching me to screw some random whore still grates on me.

I tap my temple. "Women remember everything, silly man. Quit stalling and push off the ground. It's all flat, so you just have to get used to how it feels."

Grumbling, he takes a deep breath and straightens from the bent position he was in. "If our son's first real memory is the moment I eat dirt, I'm blaming you."

I gesture toward the ground. "Technically you'd be eating pavement."

"Real reassuring, babe."

Not giving it another thought, I give him a shove and watch him teeter and roll down the narrow blacktop path. Considering he's going like two miles an hour his flailing arms make it seem like I pushed him down a hill.

"Stop flapping your arms!" I scold him.

"I'm trying!"

I shake my head and watch him jump off the board

and onto the grass. The board keeps rolling until it veers and hits a trashcan off to the side. Walking Milo and I over, I give him a blank look before bending down and retrieving my board.

"What was that?"

His lips part. "Shouldn't you be telling me that it was a good first try?"

"But was it?" I deadpan.

He rolls his eyes. "Such a critic. I bet Liam wasn't this hard on you when he showed you what to do."

Passing him the board, I go back to the stroller and play with Milo. "Now you want to talk about Liam? Has hell frozen over?"

Bringing up Liam used to be a sore subject between us. The friendship I'd shared with the Illinois native bothered Ollie, especially after my PDA moment with Liam at the skate park so many years ago.

"I'm over it," he says with a shrug.

"Because he's got a boyfriend?"

His lack of response confirms it. "Liam went easier on me, but I know you can do this without looking like I'm holding a gun to your head. Even I did better than that."

"So mean."

My bottom lip sticks out for a moment as I glance up past my lashes at him. "Sorry, I am a little off today. Maybe I need sugar."

He sets the board down. "Want to grab some food now?"

I shake my head. "We've been here for less than twenty minutes, Ollie. At least try one more time. You just need to find your balance and trust that you won't fall. If you focus on falling off, you will."

He bows at me sarcastically. "Whatever you say, Master." Stepping one foot back on the board, I move the stroller over to give him more room to push off and roll. "Speaking of which, we should do another movie marathon."

I groan. "No more *Star Wars*. Plus, we have way too many shows to catch up on. And don't think I haven't noticed you watched *The Crown* without me."

Instead of answering, he pushes off the board. If he thinks I'm not going to raise hell for betraying our pact to never watch that show without one another, he's sorely mistaken. Though my impressed nature of his limited flailing as he rolls down the pavement is worth forgetting about his indiscretions for a little while.

"You're doing it!" I praise, walking Milo along the grass as we watch Ollie. I can tell the moment the six-four man on the feminine board feels confident, because he straightens his spine and pushes again to pick up speed.

I also see a loose black lab running right toward him. Before I can even shout my warning of the barreling mutt beelining for him, they collide in a heap on the ground. The dog lands on Ollie and licks his face, wagging his tail a mile a minute before jumping off him and biting down on the skateboard.

I jog over just as the dog steals the board and trots off to wherever he came from, looking proud of the oversized stick with wheels he just collected.

I kneel beside him. "Are you okay?"

He sits up, rubbing his back. "I'm good."

We both look around for the dog, which appears next to a middle-aged woman who's also scouring the park. When her eyes land on us, she walks over, the dog on a leash beside her. I help Ollie up and brush off some pebbles from the back of his thighs.

"Stop groping me," he murmurs when my hand lingers on his butt. It's a nice one, what can I say?

The woman's eyes are dark like Ollie's and full of worry. "I'm so sorry about Oscar. He can be such a klepto sometimes." She passes me the board, covered in slobber, and then stares down at Milo. He's not paying one ounce of attention to her, even when she gushes over him. His focus is on the lab sitting with its tongue hanging out the side of his mouth.

"What a precious baby. Those eyes!" She looks between Milo and us. He still doesn't pay her any attention, instead, his blue eyes look up at mine.

"Thank you. His name is Milo."

"Milo," she repeats, wiggling her fingers.

Ollie clears his throat when he sees the stranger frown at him. "He can't hear you."

The woman straightens, her brows pinching. When realization hits her, she nods. "I see. He looks young, but

I'm sure it's never too early to start teaching him sign language."

My lips part. "Uh..." I look over at Ollie, who takes my hand. "We don't know sign language, actually."

Two dark brows draw up. "How do you communicate with him?"

It's Ollie who says, "We talk."

"But he can't hear you."

The eerily familiar tightening in my stomach reappears. Guilt. Doubt. A million other nagging feelings that weigh me down. Should we have started learning sign language? Are we inconsiderate to not think about it as soon as the doctors confirmed his condition through further diagnostic testing at the hospital?

Ollie squeezes my hand knowingly. "All due respect ma'am, but our business with our son is none of yours. In fact, we should get going."

The woman scoffs and tugs on the leash in her hand, turning the dog around and walking in the opposite direction of us.

"I know what you're thinking," he begins, taking Milo's stroller and pushing it as we walk toward the side exit, "but don't go there. That woman had no right to cast judgment."

I know he's right, but that doesn't ease my yearning to claw her eyes out and then take her dog. He seems too nice to be saddled with her the rest of his life. "Maybe..." Clearing my throat, I say, "Maybe we can stop at a library and check out some books. It wouldn't be a bad idea."

"Charlie—"

"She's not right," I agree quickly. "But I do think it would be beneficial for all of us to learn and teach Milo. I'm not backing out of the surgery. The appointment yesterday went well, and it gave me hope. All I'm saying is that he'll always be deaf. This is his life. Shouldn't we honor that?"

It doesn't take him long to think on it. "If that's what you want, then sure. We can order some books online to keep instead. Maybe see if there are videos we can watch."

I lean into his side. "Thank you."

"Does this mean I'm forgiven for watching *The Crown* without you?"

Gasping, I swat his arm. "I knew it!"

He groans loudly. "It had the Kennedy's on it, I was curious."

My arms cross over my chest. "You just wanted to drool over Jackie, didn't you? I can't believe you broke our pact."

"We can watch it tonight."

"Too late."

"Charlie." He laughs and kisses the side of my head, putting an arm around my shoulder and hugging me to him. "I love you, psycho."

I grumble, "You better."

FIVE

Ollie

The boys running laps around the gym are laughing and shoving each other as they finish their warmups before practice. I look at the watch on my wrist before blowing the whistle and waving them all over to where I stand in the middle of the court.

"Bring it in, everyone." A few of them hound each other as they settle in a circle around me. "Our first game is right around the corner, so we need to work hard the next few practices. Sage, you good to start center?"

One of the other players, Pat, instantly protests. "Come on, Coach. It's bullshit that you're keeping me out."

My brows arch. "You elbowed your own teammate in the face to get the ball. That's not how we do things around here and you know it. You're sitting out whether you like it or not."

He grumbles but doesn't argue.

Sage smiles. "I'm set, Coach James."

After going over everyone else's positions, we split off and begin practice. I don't miss the daggers Pat shoots my way but ignore him and do my job. I'm lucky this year, the junior varsity team can easily win if they set their minds to it. They just need to listen to me—something Pat likes to avoid doing. My bet is that it's a show for his friends who are also on the team. He's a good kid when he's not around other people. Maybe a little angry at the world, but I've been in his shoes before.

Halfway into practice, I tell them to take a break and grab some water. Sage and Pat are off to the side bickering, causing me to sigh and walk over before something starts.

"Problem?" I ask.

Sage looks down, Pat turns to me. "Not at all, Coach. I was just giving Sage some pointers. He was a little slow out there."

"Isn't that up for me to decide?"

Pat's cheeks color.

Sage clears his throat, grabbing his water and taking a swig before meeting my eyes. "He was just helping me out. There isn't a problem. Really."

The smile on his face is convincing enough that I let it go, but it doesn't mean I believe him fully. I know Sage and Pat hang out once in a while, but their friendship reminds me a lot like the one me and Everett had with Peter York back in high school. Basketball became competitive and we all wanted a certain place on the team. York was, and probably still is, a cocky son of a bitch who'd do anything to get what he wanted. And if or when he didn't, he lashed out.

I cross my arms over my chest. "Patrick, can I speak to you alone for a second?"

Sage's eyes widen before he quietly walks over to where some of the other guys are. Lingering gazes find their way over to us as I turn Patrick and myself away from their curious stares.

One hand on his shoulder, I speak quietly enough for only him to hear me. "I know how much you love this sport, but that's no reason to intimidate your teammate. I've been exactly where you are, kid. Worked my ass off to earn captain by the time I graduated. It got me some shit from the others. Sage doesn't deserve that just because you made a mistake."

"Coach—"

"He's your friend, isn't he?"

"Sort of. Yeah."

My head bobs. "Then act like it. You only have to sit out for one game, Pat. All I ask is that you don't act out and your spot will remain yours. Nobody else on that court needs to be treated like shit because you're upset. Get me?"

His sigh is heavy. "You were really captain of your high school team?"

That makes me smirk. "Sure was. Our team won every game but one that season."

Pat looks impressed, and the devious glint in his eyes tells me he's up to no good. "Think you still got it?"

Chuckling, I give him a loose shrug. "I suppose I have something left in me."

Pat shifts, his gaze challenging. "How about you prove it to us? The rest of practice can be you schooling us on how it's done."

I should not agree to this.

"You're on, kid."

SIX

Charlie

The gray-haired doctor bounces Milo on his lap and pats his back before glancing up at Ollie and I seated by the door.

"Are you all right, Mr. James?" Dr. Woodshed eyes the way Ollie winces as he moves on the hard chair.

I giggle. "*Mr. James* thought he could go against the JV basketball team he's coaching like he's a teenager again. They kicked his butt."

Woodshed chuckles. "It doesn't take much, does it?"

Ollie shakes his head. "It wouldn't have been so bad if I'd warmed up like they did. I'm pretty sure I tweaked something in my back."

I frown, finding his hand. "Want me to see if I can find you some Motrin?"

Woodshed pipes in. "If you have any muscle relaxers, they'd work better. It may knock you out though. They're known to do that."

A hand waves him in dismissal. "Nah. It's probably better this way. Reminds me that I'm not as limber as I used to be."

For some reason, my body comes to life over the innocent remark. He must know it too, because his knee knocks mine as a soft heat takes over my cheeks. I'm not sure what's been going on with me lately, but it's definitely sparked our sex life up. Not that it was lacking before.

I clear my throat. "So, what's next?"

It's been almost a month since we last spoke. Our insurance didn't clear the surgery, but it wouldn't stop us. We have the money, even though Ollie has been hesitant to use it. It's not that he doesn't want to, the trust fund that his father left for him is his to do what he wants with. I think he feels guilty using money he didn't earn, but with insurance denying us, our options are limited. It's almost thirty thousand dollars for an implant. Milo needs two.

Other than the minor setback with insurance, we've read up on everything there is to know about the cochlear implant. Between pamphlets, books, and websites that are Woodshed approved, we've prepared ourselves for the journey. Late nights reading in bed and early mornings at breakfast scanning papers has taught us what to look forward to.

Milo will hear.

Our voices.

Music.

Life.

It makes me teary just thinking about it.

Woodshed stands up and passes Milo to me, where I

hold him close to my chest. He takes a seat back on the rolling stool across from us. "I would like to get an outpatient surgery scheduled for the little guy. We've discussed by now that the sooner a child gets an implant, the better they'll be able to adjust and comprehend sound."

I nod. "Eighteen months, right? You told us last time that it's usually better to do it before they turn that—"

"I assure you, there isn't a switch that decreases the chances with each day following that point," Woodshed reassures with a soft smile. "It's just a pinpoint statistic because of their development. Of course, the chances of them comprehending things will become a little more difficult if they're older, but he's not at that point. His records show that he's just over fifteen months, correct?"

Ollie says, "Going on sixteen."

Woodshed stretches out his legs and rests one ankle over the other. "I checked before our appointment and saw an opening to do the surgery in two weeks. If that works for both of you, we'll pencil the little guy in. After surgery, the healing time will be about two to four weeks. Following that period will be the activation to get Milo's processor adjusted properly to fit his needs."

I nibble on the inside of my cheek, gripping Ollie's hand with mine and tightening my arm around Milo's tiny waist. "How will we know what he needs? He can't talk to tell us."

That doesn't even touch the questions regarding speech. He makes noises like any baby but hasn't been able to listen to us and learn the language patterns. I'm worried his communication will be limited from the start, even with getting him the surgery at a young age.

"We'll base it on his reactions," he says, patting my hand. "We've worked with kids around his age before. Processors can be adjusted as needed over time. There's nothing that can stop us now. Milo is in good hands."

Giving him my best smile, I lean forward and press my lips against Milo's head. He reaches up and cups my cheek, then tries shoving his fingers into my mouth. Giggling, I nibble on his little hand, which causes him to smile and bounce.

"Thank you, doctor," I find myself whispering against Milo's head.

He nods once and rolls back. "How about we get that surgery in the books, hmm? If anything comes up and it needs to be rescheduled, you have the office number. This is going to work out. I promise you."

Milo pats my cheek as I stand, almost sensing my anxiety and comforting it away. Tears blur my vision as Ollie guides us out with one hand on the small of my back. His lips peck the back of my head as we stand at reception and find out the most important date in our lives.

July sixteenth.

We both look at Milo who stares back at us adoringly. Feeling my chest fill with the oxygen it desperately needs, I try calming my racing heartbeat. Woodshed is right, Milo is in capable hands.

Soon, our lives will change forever.

SEVEN

Ollie

Watching my father play with Milo around the living room of my parents' home makes me realize just how much he's aged. Retirement has done him well, but the toll of JT Corporation over the years whitened his hair and aged his features considerably. There's no doubt in my mind that he'd do it all over again because of how much he loved founding the powerhouse that dominates the region here in New York.

Lifting Milo over his head and moving him around like a plane, my father walks over to me where my son reaches out and cups my face. I make a face, causing him to giggle and then rear back into his grandfather.

Charlie's soft murmurs coming from the kitchen are undoubtedly listing everything Bridgette James needs to know before we leave. Emergency contacts, the hotel number, what Milo is allergic to or just can't have. It's nothing my parents don't know, but this is the first time we're leaving him in the hands of someone else.

"Charlie?" I call, glancing at my watch.

Dad chuckles. "I remember those days. It's always

hard to leave them the first time around. Your mother would call every ten minutes after we left you with Darlene the first time. Trusted the woman with our lives and yours, but Bridgette had the worst separation anxiety."

My lips lift at the corners. "I don't doubt you'll be receiving texts from Charlie when I turn my back. She's been thinking about cancelling this since I suggested it."

Dad grabs my arm and squeezes. "I think it's good you two are going away before the surgery. You guys deserve it."

Milo coos and blows more spit bubbles, some of the drool landing on Dad's arm.

Charlie keeps talking with Mom, causing me to lean against the arm of the couch. "I feel bad that we're leaving. Like we should be together now more than ever."

The dark irises I get from him light up as they stare back at me. "Son, you're going to have your entire life to be with him. It extends well past eighteen years, as you can imagine. There is nothing wrong with having a day or two to yourselves, especially when there are people more than willing to help."

I nod, reaching out and tweaking Milo's little nose. My parents have been great even when I could see the confliction in their eyes when Charlie and I went public. It never deterred them to do what they could when either of us needed something. I know I could have easily asked River and Everett to look after Milo, but they have their hands full already.

"In all seriousness," Dad says, "I want to talk to you about the surgery. The cost of it has to be high with that ridiculous insurance through the school not covering it, and—"

"Dad," I groan, standing.

"The fund has been in your name since you turned twenty-one, son." His brows both raise knowingly. "Don't think I don't know you haven't touched it. You're prideful just like me. But it's meant to be used, that's why I made sure you had it."

He wanted to make sure I had money to pay for school and settle into a career and home following graduation, just like he did with River. Thankfully, my sports scholarship gave me a full ride, so I didn't have to dip into it or worry about student debt.

"I don't need it," I tell him quietly. It's a sore subject for Mom that upsets her when she hears Dad and I argue about it. They both want to know the money is going to something good, and Mom feels like there's a reason why I refuse to even touch it. No matter how many times I promise her it's not personal, hurt still lingers in her soft eyes.

His resounding sigh makes my head tip back knowing where this is leading. "Milo's surgery would be covered in full. He'd have money for schooling, college. You could buy a bigger house for the three of you. Maybe even somewhere closer—"

Our house is on the New York–Massachusetts border. While Lincoln Central School is stationed in New York, our house is just over the line by twenty minutes. It gives us enough distance from the wandering eyes that know us well in Bridgeport, yet not too much where we can't all visit each other. Both my parents, River, Everett, and their kids live just under two hours from us. We alternate who visits who, so the travel is fair.

"We like our house."

"It's a nice house." He bounces Milo, readjusting him in his arms. "I just know it would mean a lot to your mother if you were closer. She wants to be part of Milo's life more. We both do."

His point is fair, but it's not one I can justify uprooting my family for. I love my parents, but I don't love this city.

He must sense my thoughts. "People are over it, Oliver. I know it might not seem like it, but time has passed."

I shake my head in disagreement. "No offense, Dad, but you'll never understand. The second we made the choice to be together, we cemented how people here saw us. Honestly, it doesn't even matter. You know how much I wanted to move even before I met Charlie."

His shoulders loosen a little in defeat. "I admit that some webs probably shouldn't have been woven in the eyes of certain people, but I want you to know that your mother and I are happy for you. We're happy that you found Charlie and that River found Everett, even given the circumstances. We want what's best for you, and we can see that you have it. You each have beautiful families, and that makes us proud."

Rolling my neck, I give him a timid smile. We've never been one for mushy conversations, but I've spent far too long worried I've messed up any chance of hearing those words from him. It seemed like I was doomed from having the kind of relationship he would have wanted if I accepted his position at JT Corp, but I never give him the credit he fully deserves.

"Love you, Pop," I say quietly, feeling the familiar tug of emotion in the back of my throat.

He kisses Milo and tips his head. "Love you too, Oliver. Now go find your wife before she convinces Bridgette to crash here instead of leaving."

Laughing over the high probability of that actually occurring, I nod and head toward the sound of Charlie's voice.

"Hey." I kiss her cheek and then lean forward and kiss Mom's. "We need to get going. You know he'll be fine with them."

Her eyes are pleading. "I know, but—"

"Nope. Let's go."

"Ollie—"

"Nice try, babe." I gently guide her into the living room so she can say goodbye to Milo. When she picks him up and kisses him repeatedly, I worry she won't give him back.

Mom walks in and wraps an arm around my waist.

"Her love for that little boy is the purest I've ever seen, Oliver. It's precious."

My arm drapes across her shoulders. "He is her whole world. I'm lucky."

Her arm tightens. "Not her *whole* world."

Groaning, I peck the top of her head and then walk over to Charlie and Milo. It takes another few minutes, but we both finally say goodbye to everyone before I'm all but dragging her back out to the car.

When we settle in, I notice her glassy gaze directed at the house. "Baby..." I pull her into me for a tight hug. "We'll be back tomorrow afternoon, remember? It's going to be okay."

Her hand goes to her chest after she draws back into her seat. "It hurts, Ollie. It's like when..." She sniffles and wipes her cheeks. "It feels like it did after he was born. Like there's a hole. But it's not v-void like before."

Void. Following Milo's birth, Charlie struggled with post-partum depression. It was another layer of difficulty to try working past on top of his hearing loss, but she did it. She'd set up therapy appointments and talk with her doctor during checkups and do everything she could to connect with Milo despite their battles.

I weave our hands together, resting them on her thigh. "Remember how strong you are, Charlie. Our son gets his strength from you. I'm sure my parents will send pictures and videos and pick up any call you make to them. But we both know he's going to be okay. We all are. Keep reminding yourself of that."

At first, she doesn't say or do anything. Then, ever so slowly, her grip on my hand tightens and she nods.

Pulling out of the driveway, I can't help but look at the beautiful woman's profile sitting beside me. Her gaze is focused out the window as we drive away from my parents, and the raw emotion seated on her wavering lips has my heart jumpstarting in my chest.

I'm lucky.

I repeat that to myself as we near the highway.

EIGHT

Charlie

My hair sticks to my face when I lift it from the unfamiliar smelling pillowcase. Flipping onto my back, I swing my arms out and take in the fluffy bedding below me. My hip sinks into the mattress, the first reminder that I'm not home.

Peeling strands of blonde hair away from my face, I yawn and sit up to examine the dark room. I vaguely remember walking in with Ollie after checking into the hotel. As soon as he suggested I lay down for a nap, it was game over.

"Ollie?" I swing my legs over the side of the bed and walk out of the bedroom into the open living room area where Ollie is sitting on the couch.

His head instantly turns when I near the couch, his arm opening in invitation for me to cuddle into his side. "Hey, you. Sleep okay?"

My cheeks heat. "I'm sorry about that."

He kisses my temple. "You were tired, babe. You've been stressed and busy and needed the sleep. Don't apologize."

I frown and tuck my legs under me. "I know but we're supposed to be on vacation. Nothing is sexier than me drooling on the expensive looking pillows."

His chuckle makes my lips tilt upward. "I don't think there's anything that wouldn't make you sexy to me, Charlie. Pretty sure that's how we got into this whole thing."

Now my lips are spread wide, my eyes twinkling the same way his are. "You say it like it's a bad thing."

He shakes his head, moving a strand of my frizzy hair behind my ear. "Messy maybe, but not bad. We both know I wouldn't change a thing about how it happened."

Both my brows raise. "Really?"

He bites back a smile. "Maybe I would have preferred to wait until you were a little older but..."

I nudge his ribcage playfully. Causing him to laugh and catch my arm. "Thought so, Mr. Morals. But I think messy works for us."

"Oh yeah?" He grabs ahold of me and swings me over his lap so I'm straddling him. I rest my hands on his shoulders and bat my eyes innocently at him. "I think so too."

My head tilts. "You don't regret it?"

"Never."

"Not even—"

He stops me with a kiss that I happily return, parting his lips and feeling his tongue leisurely meet mine. My arms hug his neck, tugging him closer to me as I deepen the kiss and settle into his body. The muscles of his stomach contract and he groans when I grind down on his hard cock twitching under me.

"Never," he repeats, pecking my lips.

I take his bottom lip and roll it into my mouth, causing his fingers to tighten along my waist. Giggling over the ticklish sensation, I wiggle on his lap and cause him to arch his hips into me until his length is pressed right where heat is building between my legs. Our kiss starts as any other—innocent but not. Soft but demanding. It sparks something more, a yearning that neither of us can get enough of.

Even though we've said *I love you* countless times, it's these moments that cement it. It's how we show each other, how our bodies work together, how we breathe in sync with hunger and clarity.

Sometimes you need more than words.

Ollie's always given me that. He's known what I need before I do—space, comfort, everything in between. There's never been a point when I was angry at him for knowing me better than I know myself. Part of me always wondered if that's how it's meant to be with people you're meant to be with. Like there's a tether between us that's unbreakable.

My hands slowly glide down the front of his t-shirt, feeling every muscle he's worked hard for. His breathing hitches as I glide my palms under the hem and caress the skin beneath. Raising them up, up, up, I continue to kiss him like my life depends on it while brushing the slight wiry hair along his chest.

He bites down on my bottom lip when I pinch one of his nipples. "That how you want to play, little girl?" The way he growls the words at me turns me on, but not as much as when he gets my shirt off in record time and pops the button of my jeans.

I gasp playfully. "Little girl, huh? I didn't think we were doing role-play. I'm not really sure I can call you Daddy, but Uncle—"

I yelp when he flips me over on my back, instantly hovering above my body with a hungry expression on his face. It doesn't stop me from teasing him a little more, reaching between us and cupping his bulge.

"My, my." I bite my lip and begin rubbing him, feeling him grow in my hold. The heat radiating from him by the circular motions my hand makes has dampness growing between my legs. His hips arch into my touch, jerking to get more friction. "You like that idea, don't you?"

His eyes flutter closed as I squeeze him. A hushed noise sounds from the back of his throat as he leans down and nuzzles his nose against mine. Our lips hover, not quite touching but not staying away either.

"Charlie," he breathes, his lips grazing mine ever so softly. When he opens his eyes, the clarity and love staring back makes my heart thunder in my chest.

Tears well in my eyes as I move my hand to his jaw and cup it. "I know. Me too."

I love you.

I need you.

Just you.

Only you.

That's what he said during our vows, and I've felt it in my chest ever since. The words are buried deep, woven into my soul, just like he wanted them to be. A reminder. Something for when things get tough.

When our lips finally meet again, each stroke is deeper than the next. Searching. Unable to stop. He manages to peel my jeans off, along with my panties with them. He kisses his way up my body, tongue trailing along the inside of my thigh until his nose nuzzles the sensitive skin that's craving him in any form he'll give me.

"Please." I squirm when he bites down on my inner thigh, then licks away the mark he left behind until I'm seeping. "Take your clothes off, Ollie. Please?"

He doesn't stop. Instead, he moves up my leg and breathes me in until I'm panting. His tongue sweeps the seam of my lips, causing me to arch up into him. The movement has him gripping my knees and opening my legs wider to accommodate his wide shoulders while he licks me from bottom to top, sucking my clit into his mouth.

My lips part but nothing comes out as I clench fistfuls of his hair and ride out each stroke of his tongue against my clit. When he teases my entrance with one of his fingers, my entire body burns with anticipation until sweat dots my forehead. It's nothing compared to the moment his fingers and tongue both work me at the same time, two fingers plunging inside me as he keeps focused on the bundle of nerves with his mouth.

It doesn't take long before I'm riding his face, trying to get every second of pleasure I can from him. When he flattens his tongue against me, I claw at his back and spasm around him, holding on to anything I can grab.

Once my body is sated and numb, he stands up and peels off the rest of his clothes. "On your hands and knees, baby."

Legs like jelly, I obey shakily. I'm still catching my breath from what he just did, but even wetter over the idea of what's to come. When he positions himself behind me, he caresses my sides, back, and butt before thrusting inside me in one move.

"Ollie," I moan, feeling one of his hands trail up to the back of my bra, working on getting the clasps undone, while the other holds onto my hips as he jack-knifes inside of me.

"You're so fucking wet," he praises, letting the bra fall off my body, leaving me completely bare. He trails his hand around me, playing with my nipple and squeezing it, then palming my breast. "My cock is drowning in you, baby."

I move back to meet his thrusts, listening to our skin meet. I'm not embarrassed to hear how wet I am for him —my husband. In moments like this it's weird to think of him as anything other than Ollie.

But I wear his ring.

Feel his cock.

Carried his baby.

He owns me and I love it.

The hand that plays with my breast goes up to the back of my head and fists my hair. He yanks it back with minimal force, causing me to clench around him tighter. "You love this. Don't you, Charlie? Tell me how much you love it."

His cock hits me in the best way, driving me closer and closer to my second orgasm. My cheek rocks across the couch cushion, scraping against the fabric as he enters me faster. I'm sure I'll have a slight burn on my face from it, but the lick of pain is worth what he's doing to me.

"I love it so much," I whimper, feeling him twitch inside me. His grip in my hair loosens, his other palm skating to play with my clit and bring me closer to release.

"I love you," he tells me, his movements becoming jerky and chaotic as he thrusts harder and harder.

"Ollie—" I bite my wrist as he pinches my clit and makes me come around him, then feel tears prickle my eyes with oncoming emotion that hits me out of nowhere.

"Gonna come inside you, babe." Not even ten seconds after his warning, he spills himself into me, holding my hips against him as his orgasm settles.

He pulls out and carefully rests me down so he's spooning me. One of his arms wraps around the back of my head that I use as a pillow, the other wrapping around my waist to hold me against his warm body.

A tear I didn't know got pass my defenses slides down my cheek before I can stop it and lands on Ollie's arm.

"Charlie?" His arm tenses around me before he guides me to turn onto my back. Sitting up on one arm, he stares down at me. "Did I get too rough? Shit, I'm—"

"No." My voice cracks. I shake my head and try smiling. "I'm sorry. I've just been emotional lately. You didn't hurt me, I promise."

His thumbs wipe at my damp cheek. "It's understandable why you would be. How about I order us room service? We'll junk out and rent a movie or something."

I sniffle. "Like ... porn?"

His chuckle shakes me. "I meant like an actual movie, but I'm down with that if you are."

I roll my eyes and playfully swat him, sitting up and wiping at my own cheeks. "I'm good with just a movie, thank you very much. And ice cream."

His brows pinch. "No donuts?"

I deadpan. "I doubt room service has donuts, Ollie. But I'm pretty sure they'll have ice cream. Vanilla. Extra chocolate syrup."

He stares at me for way longer than I expect, before slowly nodding. I'm not sure what crosses his mind but it doesn't stop him from picking up his cell and dialing the number on the room service card left on the glass coffee table in front of the couch.

Biting my lip, I watch the muscles of his back move as he reaches for his discarded clothes on the ground and gives our orders. When he hangs up, I'm on my knees and kissing the back of his neck, trailing my lips to the crook of it and biting down to mark him.

"Again?" His voice is husky.

I reach forward and grip his already hard cock, squeezing it before jerking my palm up and down until he's leaning into me. "Doesn't seem like little Ollie disagrees."

He turns his head and captures my lips, brushing the side of my face with his hand and pulls away. "Please don't call my cock that."

I lick his bottom lip. "Sorry, Uncle Ollie."

He groans.

I giggle.

Nothing changes.

NINE

Ollie

I'm one lucky bastard.

My front teeth dig into my bottom lip, dragging it inward as Charlie smooths out the black material that clings to her body. Her fingers run through her hair as she examines herself in the mirror. The curves that sculpt her are more pronounced in the form-fitting dress, especially when she turns and reveals the ass I'm caught staring at.

"Do I look okay?" The fact she even has to ask makes me feel like I've failed her somehow.

Walking over, I glide my hands down the curve of her waist before pulling her into me. "I want to rip that dress off and then fuck you against the wall, if that's any indication of how you look." Instead of doing that, I peck her lips and shake my head. "You're gorgeous."

Her cheeks pinken as she steps back. "I wasn't sure where you're taking me, but you mentioned somewhere nice..."

My lips tilt. She's been trying to get information out of me all morning since I mentioned that we had plans before going back to Bridgeport for Milo. Besides hinting that she should dress up, I gave nothing else away.

"You're going to love it. Promise."

Her nose scrunches. "You know I'm not a hug fan of—"

I silence her with another kiss, this one much longer than the one before. Palms greet my hips, resting on the soft material of my blue button-up that I haven't worn in years. Neither of us are typically the type to dress up and go out, but I know today is all about Charlie. We're going back to a time when she didn't second guess if she looked okay or appropriate, or worried about anyone other than herself.

Caressing her cheek, I withdraw from her welcoming body and offer her my arm. She doesn't hesitate to take it, letting me walk her out of the bedroom and toward where our shoes rest by the couch.

She nibbles on her lip. "Ollie?"

"Hmm?"

She squats and picks up the black Converse, studying them indecisively. "I didn't think to bring any other shoes. These are—"

"Perfect."

She blinks up at me.

I nod. "Put 'em on. We'll be late."

Warily, she slides into them and flattens out the wrinkles of her dress once she's finished. I can tell by the way she tugs on the hem that she's nervous. Ever since she had Milo, she's been cautious about what she wears and how much skin she exposes. All thanks to some bitch in the store shortly after he was born who commented on a pair of shorts she wore. It's been a long time since I punched someone, but I was two seconds away from launching produce at the woman who felt the need to degrade my wife.

"You're really not going to tell me?" she asks again once we're in the car.

Her body is angled carefully in my direction, her eyes wide and pleading. Despite it all, I wink and say, "Nope."

She groans and leans back, staring out the windshield at the scenery we pass. It isn't a long drive before we're pulling into a tiny cobblestone establishment. The outside does no justice for the intimate restaurant inside and gives nothing away other than the promise of fine dining.

Hesitantly, she unbuckles and follows my lead. Getting out and rounding the front of our car, I reach for her and she quickly cups her palm with mine. I guide us to the glass doors that are covered by an auburn canopy that matches the curtains lining the windows.

As soon as the door opens, we're greeted by the faintest smell of fresh bread. Charlie squeezes my hand when we stop by the hostess station, taking in the wooden interior that's dimly lit by candles and threaded white lights. There's a large bar off to the right lined with wooden stools, and tables and chairs of the same material scattered throughout the rest of the room.

In the background is the softest sound of classical

music drifting from the speakers. When the owner walks out from the back with a big smile to go along with his expensive tuxedo, I let go of Charlie's hand and meet him halfway to shake his.

"Mr. James," he greets, nodding his head. His eyes drift from me to Charlie, his smile softening a little. "Mrs. James. I've heard great things about you."

Charlie blinks and looks at me, her face tinting pink like it usually does when people compliment her. She gives him a timid smile and walks over to me, holding out her hand. "Thank you, Mr...."

He clasps hers gently. "You can call me Mark, sweetheart."

"Charlie."

They let go of each other and I wind an arm around Charlie's waist. "Look to your left, all the way in the back."

She does as I say, turning and focusing the grand piano stationed in the corner. There are candles around it, making the sleek black paint glow. The sharp inhale I hear from her makes me lean forward and smile into the side of her hair. Her fingers find mine and squeeze.

It's Mark who says, "The afternoon crowd will be here in about forty minutes. It doesn't get too packed, but we get a fair amount of people. They love live music."

Charlie gawks at him. "You ... you'd let me play?"

He bobs his head. "Mr. James—"

"Oliver," I correct.

"—raved about what a brilliant pianist you are. I'd be

honored if you played. First, we have a special lunch for the two of you. The restaurant doesn't open until noon, so it'll be intimate."

Charlie's hand tightens. "Wow. I don't know what to say." Her voice is a whisper as she looks up at me. "You did all this for me?"

My lips spread into a warm smile. "You deserve this, Charlie. You've been so caught up in making sure Milo is okay, but now is your chance to do what you love."

Emotion washes over her face, causing her lips to waver from the awed smile she gives me. I can tell she wants to say something but doesn't have the words. I just nod once to let her know I understand.

Mark shows us to a table near the piano, stationed next to the window that looks out into a large garden. He pushes in Charlie's chair and tells us our waiter will be out in a moment.

When it's just us again, she just stares at me and shakes her head. I nudge her foot with mine under the table. "What? I know you don't like surprises, but—"

"I love this." Her voice cracks, so she clears it and drapes the auburn cloth napkin on her lap. "Sometimes I wonder what I did to deserve you, Oliver James. I feel like I owe someone for bringing you to me."

I lean forward and reach for her hand. "I think we both know it's the other way around. I'd do anything for you, Charlie. There's no doubt in my mind that we're meant to be in for the long haul. Look at the risks we took."

"*You* took the risks. I just ... took."

I wink at her. "And I gave."

Her teeth sink into her bottom lip.

"Point is," I say, "is that we deserve each other. It doesn't matter what we have or haven't done. Agreed?"

She nods. "You brought me here to play."

"I did." I gesture toward the plate. "And eat, of course. Mark Jefferson's grandson was on the basketball team at Lincoln a couple years ago. He's mentioned me coming here a few times, and I figured now was good as any."

"And he doesn't mind me playing?"

I chuckle. "Trust me, Mark wouldn't say yes unless he wanted to. In fact, he's been trying to get you to come here and play ever since I mentioned you could."

Her brows arch up. "You talk about me a lot, huh?"

The waiter comes just then and gives us their specials, which we order two of along with some sweat tea. When he leaves for the kitchen again, I lean back in my chair.

"Mark's wife used to be a pianist."

She catches the past tense use of words quickly, letting her eyes dim over someone she doesn't even know. It's so ... Charlie. "When I mentioned you played, he told me you should come here and give a performance. I know you play for Milo, but you love performing."

Her throat bobs. "I didn't think of anything to give you."

My hand swipes at the slow smirk spreading across my face. "I'd say you've given me quite a bit lately."

"Ollie!" Humor dances in her eyes, making the green more vibrant. "Behave, we're in public."

I nod slowly, looking around the empty room before meeting her gaze again. "You're right. Wouldn't want the other patrons to hear."

She rolls her eyes. "I wonder what Milo will be like when he's older with parents like us."

"Amazing," I state confidently. "Caring. Loving. Selfless. Confident. Talented. I can keep going, but I think you get the point."

The cloth on her lap captures her focus as she toys with the threaded ends. "I'm sure you're right, but sometimes..." Her shoulders lift. "I can't help but worry."

"It's normal."

"He'll be able to hear soon," she whispers, in awe of the realization.

The surgery date is nearing quickly, the rest of May having gone by in no time and June passing even quicker. Even though it's outpatient, she's packed and repacked a bag for him at least three times. She's reread information on what to expect, googled everything she'd possibly need to know, and called Dr. Woodshed countless times with questions she already knows the answer to.

"Nothing will stop him." A tiny smile forms at the corners of her lips.

"Nothing," I agree.

Lunch is accompanied by conversations about the sign language classes we've taken over the past few weeks. We both show Milo what we've learned as we go, and Charlie insists he's even mimicked her before when she was showing him the alphabet. His attentiveness to everything she does makes it seem possible. He picks up on the way she teaches him to feel the vibrations in the piano, to hit certain keys, and everything in between.

Milo is smart. There's no doubt he'll pick up the language easily, no matter the form he's taught it in. Dr. Woodshed mentioned the necessity for special therapy to help him learn speech, on top of extra schooling to allow him to adjust. He'll pick it up without a hitch, I'm certain of it.

Mark shows up shortly before the doors officially open, gesturing for Charlie to situate herself at the piano when she's ready. The cake we split between us is nothing but crumbs, and I can tell Charlie doesn't want to waste another second before sitting on that bench.

"Go." I tip my chin. "I'll be watching."

She stands and walks over to me, bending to give me a chaste kiss before moving her lips to my ear. "You better know a private place to park after we leave here, because there's no way I'll be able to wait until we're back at the hotel."

My cocks instantly stiffens at her words, fire shooting down my limbs as she pulls away. The little vixen in the tight dress saunters away with confidence, but I know it's just her being her. Blindly beautiful, simply breathtaking.

And when she sits down at the bench after studying the keyboard, the very first song she plays as people spill in is ours.

We lock eyes the entire time, never once missing the emotion swirling between us through every note. I remember the first time she played it for me, how I had to say goodbye because I needed to give her time. Space. Independence. She'd asked me if I'd love her despite her flaws and scars and past.

The answer was always yes, even when I let the door close behind me that afternoon.

Can you love me anyway, Ollie?

I mouth, "*Always*."

TEN

Charlie

ANXIETY RIPPLES THROUGH ME AS I HOLD MILO CLOSE to my chest in the waiting room. The squirming bundle on my lap has no idea where we are, why we're here, or that his life is about to change forever. In fact, none of the kids in the playroom seem to have a clue why they're there.

I bounce my knees, partially to sooth him but also because I can't stop fidgeting. The tightening in my chest makes it hard to breathe, and my temples ache more every time the double doors open for patients to be called back by the nurses in blue scrubs.

Ollie rests his palm on my knee. "Deep breaths, baby. Everything is going to be okay."

A young red-headed woman sitting across from us smiles. "First time?"

I wince. "There will be more?"

The sympathy on her face is clear. "Well, hopefully not surgeries. But trust me, you'll find yourself at the hospital with them as they get older. Stomachaches, stitches, flus, you name it."

My eyes widen as I stare at Ollie.

He just shrugs. "She's got a point. Look at how many times River and Everett brought one of theirs in."

I brush a hand through Milo's blond locks, trying to comfort myself in its softness. "I know, but I kind of hope that won't be us."

Both Ollie and the woman laugh softly over my naïve hope. I notice the little girl who can't be more than three playing with some dolls by the stranger's feet. She's all smiles as she lives in her little fantasy world.

"What's your daughter in for?" I ask, hoping it'll help ease some of my worry. I tell myself that everyone here is probably going through the same thought processes as me.

The woman shifts in the chair. "Oh, she's not…" She clears her throat, smiling. "She's in to get her tonsils removed."

A man walks over to them, causing the little girl to shoot up and wrap herself around his legs. He instantly picks her up hugs her tightly, her little arms wrapping around his neck.

"Daddy," she croaks. "I feel funny."

He rubs her back. "I know, sweetie. We're going to get you all better. And you know what? You get to eat ice cream and Jell-O for a few days. How cool is that?"

The woman we were talking to smiles at them in adoration, but there's something I know all too well in her eyes. Longing. And based on her hesitation over me calling the little girl hers, my bet is that she's not.

Peeling her eyes away from the burly man who takes

the seat next to her, she looks between me and Ollie. "What's your little guy in for?"

Deafness seems to be a sore spot for a lot of people which I can never understand. Any time we bring up Milo's condition, it's like they want to either give us their opinion on what to do or judge us like we did something wrong to cause it. It's made me cautious to make friends with people in our neighborhood who have kids, because the last thing I want is unwarranted, degrading advice.

"He's getting a cochlear implant," I answer, holding him a little tighter.

Her eyes soften, and a friendly smile appears back on her face. "That's amazing. I bet you two are excited."

It's Ollie who admits, "More nervous than anything, if we're being honest."

Her response is instant. "Oh, I'm sure. I just about had a breakdown when I heard that Ainsley needed to have the procedure." She looks at the little girl, whose eyes are closed as she rests on her father's shoulder. "It's tough going through this."

"I'll say," I whisper, kissing the back of Milo's head. He tips his head back and smiles at me, clapping his hands. I giggle. "Yeah? You must be excited too."

He does his little wiggle, making Ollie and I chuckle. The woman lets out a soft sigh and watches as Milo reaches up and tugs on a strand of my loose hair.

"He's adorable," she compliments.

I get my hair back. "Thank you. Ainsley is gorgeous

too. She looks a lot like her dad." And it's true. From what I can see, her complexion is identical to his. Her hair is slightly different than his dirty blond, almost a strawberry tone, but still close.

"I'm Piper by the way."

Ollie tips his head. "I'm Oliver. This is my wife Charlie, and our little guy is Milo."

"What a cute name!"

The man chuckles. "Getting baby fever, Pipe? Thought you said you'd only spoil your godchildren and live with fifty cats."

Piper's cheeks burn red. "You have to admit that their baby is adorable, Danny. Look at him! But, yes. I plan to spoil Ainsley rotten. She's already got something waiting at the house for when she's better."

The man, Danny, shakes his head with an amused smile on his face. "You're one of a kind."

I watch them with interest, wondering what their story is. It's not my business, but it keeps my mind from wandering places I don't want it to.

Before anything else can be said, the double doors open, and Milo's name is called by a young man. Panic instantly settles into my bones, and I'm tempted to make a break for it before they can take him from me.

Ollie stands and gives me his hand.

I stare.

"Charlie," he encourages. "It's time."

The male nurse walks over with a smile, holding a

tiny band for Milo's wrist. "Good morning. I'm Devon and I'll be taking you into to pre-op. I just need to verify Milo's name and date of birth."

I'm still sitting, blinking between the men staring at me. "Uh ... Milo Brahm James." My voice gets shaky as tears well in my eyes.

Ollie fills in the rest of the needed information, giving me a chance to take a deep breath and stand.

It's going to be worth it.

I chant that a few more times before we're guided in the back, one of Ollie's hands firmly but gently planted on the small of my back like he knows what I was thinking of doing.

When we're given a room and told to get Milo changed into the proper gown, my hands shake too much. Ollie takes charge, cooing and praising Milo who just keeps smiling and looking around with curiosity.

I grip the counter and watch them—the two most important people in my life. They're both carefree right now. At least, Ollie plays the part. I know he's worried, but one of us needs to be emotionally stable. Unfortunately, that's not me at the moment.

"Breathe," he reminds me, holding Milo and walking over to me. "Look at how handsome he is. Don't you think so, Mommy?"

"Please don't call me that."

He scoffs. "I meant it in a non-creepy way, mother of my child. But if you insist."

I take Milo from him as we wait for the doctor to come in and confirm the procedure happening so we can fill out the final forms.

Evening my breathing, I push past the lightheadedness and focus on Milo. On his bright eyes and wide smile and natural beauty. We created a masterpiece, Ollie and me.

"You're so beautiful, baby boy," I whisper, nuzzling my nose into his cheek. His giggle eases some of the stress, but it doesn't last long when the curtain opens, and the doctor announces himself.

It goes exactly as we've been told.

Talking and paperwork.

More talking.

More paperwork.

Ollie handles signing all the papers while I cuddle Milo until I know I need to pass him along. The thought of watching them take him into the back consumes me until tears can't help but roll down my face.

"Mrs. James," Dr. Woodshed comforts.

"I know, I know. He'll be fine. But..."

Ollie grabs a tissue from the counter and dabs my cheeks, leaning in to kiss my temple. "I know what you're feeling right now, but we'll get through this. Okay, baby? We're strong. Milo is strong. Remember that."

We're strong.

Milo is strong.

I nod and hold my breath when they announce

they're ready for him. My hands begin shaking as I give Milo another kiss and hug before passing him to Ollie to do the same.

"You be good back there, champ." Only I seem to hear the tiniest crack in his words as he swallows his emotion. Milo watches us with my awareness as he's passed into one of the nurse's arms. When I see his eyes glaze, I suddenly feel like the worst parent alive.

"W-Wait. Maybe—"

"Charlie." Ollie puts his hand on my arm.

The curtain opens.

They walk out.

And I breakdown.

Ollie pulls me into his arms, hushing me and combing his fingers through my hair. But I can hear the familiar muffled cries even from here as they take him back and feel my knees buckle under me.

The room spins as nausea sweeps through me and Ollie curses before pulling me onto the bed for balance. "Charlie? Baby?"

My vision blurs as I choke for air.

"Sir? Is she okay?"

"I..." Ollie's hand finds mine. "I don't know. She looks like she's about to pass out. The stress has been tough on her."

Brushing it off, I try standing but the lightheaded feeling I have doubles. I try telling Ollie I'm fine, that I haven't eaten because of nerves, but don't get anything out before everything blackens.

. . .

SOMETHING WARM TOUCHES MY HAND, WRAPPING around my fingers and tightening. My eyelids flutter open, adjusting to the light before meeting a pair of dark brown eyes.

His smile is warm, but there's something else mixed into it. Whatever it is, it's light. Not necessarily worried, which I expected but am certainly glad about.

"Hey. Are you doing all right?"

I nod, sitting up with his help. "How long was I out? I'm so—"

"Don't." He shakes his head and takes my hand, kissing the back of it. "You've only been out for about eight minutes. No need to apologize. The nurse drew some blood just to be sure everything is all right, but you're in pristine shape."

"It was just stress. I didn't eat..." I glance at the little circular band aid where they must have taken the blood.

"You really need to eat, Charlie."

"I was nervous—"

"I know." He squeezes my hand. "Trust me, babe. I know you were. But..." His lips twitch with a wavering smile that makes me narrow my eyes suspiciously at him.

Managing to swing my legs over the side of the bed, I sigh. "Why are you being weird? I promise I'm fine."

His palm cups my knee. "I asked them to let me tell you before they came in again to see how you're doing." He squeezes me. "You're pregnant, Charlie."

My lips part.

He pauses, his smile a little smaller. "Did you hear me?"

I blink. "Yeah. Definitely heard you." Trying to take a deep breath and calculate when my last period was, I shake my head in a daze. "I don't know what to say."

The wince he gives me makes me frown. He's happy over this news. Am I? It isn't that I'm *not* happy over being pregnant. But...

"I'm sorry," I whisper, palming my eyes and trying to breathe. "I don't remember missing any of my pills. It's just a surprise is all."

"Do you not want...?" He doesn't finish the sentence, uncertainty lingering in his words like he's afraid of my reply.

I quickly grab his hand. "No, it's not that. We've talked about having another kid eventually, but I didn't expect it to be so soon. And we're going through things with Milo, *big* things, and it's all so much."

Emotion clogs my chest as new panic seeps into my skin. What were we thinking? I honestly had no idea I was pregnant. My periods have always been irregular—I'd miss some months and get two during others. I just assumed it'd been finicky again.

"I'm excited about this," he admits, looking genuinely ecstatic despite his wariness over my reaction. "But I understand that the timing could have been better. Things happen for a reason though, don't they? We've always said that. I believe it."

I wet my lips and find myself nodding. "I do too. I just..." How can I explain to him that I'm worried? My post-partum depression left me disconnected with Milo for a long time when he loved me unconditionally. It isn't easy putting that concern to words, knowing Ollie can't possibly understand what it's like to feel the way I do. When Milo needed me, I distanced myself, battled myself, and I haven't quite forgiven myself for it.

What if I feel that way again? I had spent months looking forward to holding Milo, only to want nothing to do with him when he was finally in the world. What kind of mother is like that? I still think about how broken I felt—the kind of broken I'd never felt before. I always promised myself if I had kids, I'd treat them differently than my own biological parents treated me. They chose drugs, sex, anything but their own daughter. Looking back now, I know I'd never become them. But feeling the disconnect I did for a long time before getting the proper help made me feel no different than them.

Ollie's touch is soothing. "Do you think there will be more health complications?"

My shoulders lift slightly. "That's part of it. We never know what will happen, Ollie. I know Milo isn't broken because of his impairment, but things will be really tough on him growing up. There are things we can't protect him from."

"Just because it happened with one doesn't mean it'll happen again," he reminds me, caressing my knee with his thumb. "And there will always be different things parents can't protect their kids from, Charlie. That's life. Even if this does happen again, look at us. We're taking care of it. We're looking out for Milo. Everything is fine."

He has a point I can't argue.

"Look at me," he commands, his touch tightening a little. I obey. "I know things have been tough. There will always be bad days, right? We've both gone through them, but we've also come out on top every time. Milo is no exception, and our new baby won't be either."

The curtain opens before I can answer, and the same nurse who came in earlier greets me with a happy smile. "I'm glad to see you're awake, Mrs. James. How are you feeling?"

"Better." I clear my throat. "I wouldn't mind some water though, if that's okay."

She nods once. "I can grab you some in just a minute. Did you speak with your husband about the blood test we took?"

My head still doesn't wrap around the results, but I bob my head. "I'm pregnant."

"Congratulations." She glances down at a folder in her arms. "The doctor who looked over your labs mentioned seeing if you're interested scheduling an appointment with Women's Health since this is your primary hospital. I can get something set up now for you."

"That would be great." I look at Ollie for a moment, then back at the nurse. "I wouldn't be able to get seen by Radiology for an ultrasound today, would I?"

The apologetic expression she casts tells me the answer before she verbalizes it. "I'm sorry, but that department is usually pretty busy. Women's Health has been great with appointments though, so you'd be seen within the next week. It'd be faster than trying to get a tech to do one for you in Radiology."

I just nod and agree to have her schedule something, knowing she's right. Part of me just wants to know the answers. How is the baby? How far along am I? Does everything look okay?

My palm rests on my stomach. "This is nuts. Don't you think so?"

"I think it's amazing," Ollie says.

I tilt my head, studying the way he stares at my stomach with the biggest smile on his face. "You really think that, huh?"

He meets my eyes. "I get to spend the rest of my life with my best friend, Charlie. Not only that, but you've given me children. How can I not think that's amazing?"

My heart soaks up every word. When the nurse comes back with a cup of ice water and an appointment card with a date and time printed on the top, I thank her.

She tips her head. "If you're feeling all right, I can take you to the surgical waiting room. When Milo is finished, someone will come to let you know. The number on his band matches the one on the paperwork you were given, and you can track the progress—when he's out and in the Recovery room—on the television in there, so you know what's going on."

When we're in the small little room with rows of chairs and other families, I hold onto Ollie's hand and search the screen for Milo's number. Each step of the surgical process is color coded. His is green. Surgery. When it turns purple then we'll know he's out and in Recovery.

"Why does this feel unreal?" I whisper, leaning my cheek on his shoulder.

"Because we're happy," he answers almost instantly. "Sometimes happiness feels like it's too good to be true."

I nibble on my lip, hefting a sigh. "I am. Happy, I mean. I know my reaction didn't seem like it, but a baby..." I play with the ring on his finger, almost in awe. "It's crazy but it's what I want. Maybe a girl."

He chokes. "Uh..."

I sit up. "You don't want a girl?"

He physically pales. "It's not that I don't want one, but..." His shoulders tense. "I'll feel more helpless than I already do if we have a girl. I know boys. Why do I feel like it'd be karma if it'd be a girl?"

I giggle. "You'd be overprotective."

He hums.

"Like Everett," I add.

He chuckles. "He'd have a fucking field day over it, wouldn't he? Can't say I blame him. Never did."

"Don't start with that."

Lips pressing into a firm line, he gives me a quick

glance before exhaling heavily through his nose. "It's in the past now. It just gets me thinking about what I'd do in the situation. If we have a daughter and she gets involved with someone older than her, I'd..."

"You would what?"

"I'd lose it."

Like Everett did. "Trust me, I get it. But we can't be hypocrites either. How would that make us look as parents?"

One brow arches. "Good?"

I roll my eyes. "I mean, sure. Probably not in her eyes, but we'd be winning. Rational, even."

"Ah." He clicks his tongue. "We weren't very rational for a while, were we? Looking back from a new perspective—"

"The perspective hasn't changed," I cut him off, sitting up to look at him. "Time may have, but we haven't. Our past is *ours*. It's messy and ugly and perfectly imperfect. It's *us*. And you know what? I hope both Milo and baby number two get to experience lives like that."

His cringe tells me he disagrees.

"Think about it, Ollie." I put my hand on his chest, right over his heart. "Think about what it would be like if we hadn't gone through what we did. Nothing came easy, and it made us stronger for it. We want them to be strong, don't we? Any parent would."

His hand covers mine, pressing it against his heartbeat. I absorb the rhythm, getting lost in its melody like I've done countless times before. I'd fall asleep to it, knowing I'd wake up to it the very next day and repeat it all again.

He relents. "You're right."

I smile. "I know I am."

His laugh is low, amused. "The thought of a girl still terrifies me in case you were wondering. But I'd be happy."

The truth spills so easily off my tongue for the world to hear. "Me too, Ollie. Me too."

I'm not sure how we manage to keep conversation going long enough to pass the time, but as I'm digging into donut number two that Ollie bought me from the hospital café down the hall, our names are called by a dark-skinned man at the door.

My eyes quickly dart to the screen.

Purple.

We both meet him at the door, where he reaches out and shakes our hands. "I want to let you know that Milo is settled in Recovery and should wake up soon. It's policy that only one person comes in at a time, but since he's so young you both can. I'm sure he'll be happy to see you."

Tears well in my eyes that I quickly blink away as we follow him to the new unit our baby is resting in. Ollie holds my hand, which I grip so tight his skin turns white. He doesn't comment on it, just lets me do what I need to seek comfort.

Stuffing what's left of my donut into a napkin in my purse, the man opens the door for us and gestures toward the third green curtain off to the right. My feet carry me quickly into the little room, where a nurse is checking over his vitals.

In the middle of a large white bed is our precious baby laying on his stomach. His hands are sprawled out to his sides, his legs kicked out so he's taking up as much room as possible. The sight of his torso rising and lowering with each breath slowly makes one lone tear fall down my cheek.

Ollie notices and brushes it away with his thumb, kissing my temple and guiding us over to Milo. "See, Charlie? He's okay."

Wrapped around his head is white gauze with little orange striped designs. Seeing him like this does ease some f the worry I'd obsessed over, but the gauze feeds what remains. But Ollie is right. Milo is out of surgery and okay.

The biggest step is complete.

Shortly after we settle into chairs by his bed, Dr. Woodshed comes in and tells us how well the surgery went. He doesn't hesitate to answer questions we sprout out him even though they're ones we've asked hundreds of times.

Well, I did anyway.

"My biggest suggestion?" Woodshed says, standing from the stool by the curtain. "Go out as a family in about a week. Give him a little time to recover from surgery, then plan a trip. In no time, he'll be ready to come see us again and get the processer adjusted."

"It'll be okay if we do that?" I ask.

Woodshed nods. "Like any surgery, it's about keeping an eye on the surgical site. We'll make a post-op appointment for two weeks from now where I'll see how the little guy is doing. But no, I don't see any problems with taking him anywhere. In fact, I encourage it. It can be a treat for him, a reward even for being so good."

Ollie shakes the doctor's hand again. "I can't thank you enough."

Woodshed waves it off. "I'm just doing my job, son. But you and your wife are more than welcome. I'll see you both soon."

My eyes focus on Milo as his little hands begin moving, followed by the softest noise. I'm by his side in a matter of seconds, reaching down and touching his hand so he knows I'm here.

The cry he lets out causes me to rub his back in circles like I do when he gets antsy. Ollie takes his other hand which Milo responds to quickly. His eyes open groggily like they do after a good night's sleep, searching the room before seeing us beside the bed.

"Hi, sweetheart," I coo, giving his back a little pat, causing him to yawn. "I hear you were so brave in there."

His eyes move to Ollie. "Love you, buddy. We're going to get you home soon, okay?"

Milo squirms and reaches out, causing me to react instantaneously. I pick him up carefully and bounce him in my arms while making more circular motions on his back. Normally his hands will go to my hair and tug, but

I can tell the medicine has him drowsy. He rests his cheek against my shoulder and let's his arms wrap loosely around my neck.

"I love you," I whisper.

I can't wait for the day he can hear it.

ELEVEN

Ollie

Once upon a time I wondered if I'd get the life so many others had. One filled with love, happiness, and things to look forward to. Considering how I grew up, the opportunities I had thanks to my parents, I was being ungrateful.

Before my depression diagnosis and therapy, I'd realized I wasn't being ungrateful at all. I was searching for the things I watched everyone obtain easily. When Charlie came into my life, it clicked in place.

All of it.

And now, seeing the familiar curve of her stomach that seemingly popped overnight, I realize that I just needed to wait for the right person. It's been a month since Milo's surgery. In that time, we found out Charlie is almost done with her first trimester, leaving us both surprised over how far along she is. What I didn't tell her is that I suspected it—the mood swings, hormones, and food cravings were all there. Still, it seems like we have even less time to prepare for a second child. We have the room, but the space isn't kid appropriate. The walls are too bland, and the furniture is minimal.

Between planning to announce her pregnancy and making sure Milo is healing well, we've been busy. Since getting the all-clear from Woodshed, we've gone on little outings with Milo to celebrate. In a matter of days, we'll be able to go back in and watch our baby move on to the final phase of the process.

Charlie pulls me away from my thoughts with a small nudge to my side. "Should we be alarmed that our son is more interested in the lion cage than the cute penguins?"

Milo has been more attentive during our trip past the lion exhibit at the local zoo than anything else we've seen.

"We should get him a cat," she concludes.

Chuckling, I say, "*Him*, huh?"

She bats her lashes at me. "There are studies that show the benefits of children growing up with pets. Seems like he loves cats, so it seems logical."

"Just admit you want a cat, Charlie."

"*Milo* wants a cat," she insists.

I shake my head and keep pushing the stroller, moving on to the tiger habitat. There are a few more people around the glass watching as one of the large cats jumps onto a log and perches.

"See!" Charlie gestures to Milo, who reaches out with his little finger, pointing at the tigers. "Come on, you have to admit he acts like he likes them."

Sighing, I agree. "We'll talk about it more later. We have enough to think about, don't you think?"

Her bottom lip sticks out. "But what if I told you there are kittens up for adoption at that shelter near the school? Orange ones, Ollie!"

I blink. "And you say it's Milo who wants a cat. Did he show you the adoption flyers too?"

"We can get a boy and name him Tony."

I stop walking. "Like the tiger?"

Her expression screams *duh*.

"Isn't that..." I make a face. "I don't know, a little unoriginal?"

She gasps. "Unoriginal would be me calling it Garfield. Let's be real, Oliver James. Anyone who gets an orange cat thinks about naming it Garfield."

"Or Tony," I add just to tease her.

Her groan is cute, making it hard to hide my amused smile. "Fine. What about Cheeto? I think that would be a cool name."

"Like I said, we'll talk about it later."

"Ollie!"

"Charlie." I laugh. "I'm trying to be logical here. We've got a baby on the way. That and Milo's journey should be our main focus."

I can tell she agrees by the way her expression softens. It's cute how badly she wants a cat, for Milo and her, but I'm worried we're adding too much to our plate.

"Hey." I reach out and brush her arm. "I want to give you the world, Charlie. One day, we'll expand. If you want a cat, we'll get a cat. If you want a dog, we'll get a dog. Hell, a hamster? Game on. But right now, we need to focus on the kids. On us. On our family."

All she has to say is, "Our cat would eat the hamster, Ollie. Duh." And somehow I fall a little more in love with her.

Pushing the stroller further past the various feline habitats, I can't help but notice how both Milo's and Charlie's faces light up. It doesn't take long to know I'm in a losing battle. Before I know it, I'll be house training a cat and replaced in bed by the furry thing.

The furry thing named *Cheeto*.

"What are you thinking about?" My not-so-innocent wife asks.

Shaking my head, I study the people we pass and give a few of them a small smile and head nod in greeting. "Nothing of importance."

"Liar."

I just hum and watch the animals.

"We're getting a cat, aren't we?"

Nothing.

"We totally are."

Silence.

"Is now a good time to tell you that the shelter is expecting us on Wednesday afternoon?"

When I finally look at her again, she smiles that beautiful fucking smile that makes it hard to be upset. As annoying as she can be, I love her. Unconditionally. I'm

B. CELESTE

probably lucky she didn't just adopt a cat and hide it in the music room before telling me.

"You're something else, Charlie." I grin to myself and this world we've created. The world I questioned I'd get to experience when I was at my lowest.

When I get to those moments, the ones I struggle pulling myself from, all I need to remember is this image. The one of the glowing woman with vibrant blonde hair, and a tiny blond baby to match.

Both smiling.

Both pure.

Both ... mine.

TWELVE

Charlie

The anticipation weaves itself into every fiber of my being as we watch Milo play with some of the plush kid toys Woodshed provides in his little office. There are computers and wires everywhere, making the moment surreal. Ollie keeps one hand on my back at all times, while the other rubs Milo's arm.

"Okay," Woodshed, says, rolling over to us with tiny hearing aids in his hands. "Keep in mind these ear molds will need to be replaced every month or two as he grows up. We've talked about cost before, and these will certainly add up after a while since his ears will develop with time. The hospital does have a program to assist families with hearing impaired children if worst comes to worst."

Ollie's hand stops caressing my back. "I appreciate that, doctor. We're covered though."

Woodshed simply nods and smiles. "Are you ready? I'm going to put these in and then play around with the various settings. What I want you to do is talk quietly to him. I'll intervene and try getting his attention to see if he can hear from both processors. Okay?"

It's hard to swallow, much less talk, so all I do is bob my head up and down. Ollie's hand rounds my shoulder and squeezes in comfort. His body tenses beside me as Woodshed places the earpieces. Milo wiggles and tries capturing his hand, causing us all to chuckle over his curiosity. When he's all finished, Woodshed rolls back to his computer and clicks on a few things.

"Ready?" Ollie and I nod. "I'm turning them on in three, two, one..." The mouse clicks one final time before our eyes lower to Milo.

Woodshed gestures for us to talk.

I take a deep breath. "Milo?"

Milo continues playing without any reaction to my voice. My eyes meet Woodshed's, who gives me a reassuring smile.

"Don't get discouraged. I'll keep turning the volume up a little more each time until he can hear you. Just take a deep breath and talk to him."

He adjusts the sound and nods at me.

"Milo?" My voice breaks a little, so I clear it and tell myself that Woodshed is right. I can't get discouraged if the first few volumes don't work.

Ollie kisses Milo's head. "Buddy? Can you hear us?"

Nothing.

Woodshed adjusts it again, waving his hand at us for a third time. When I put my hand on Milo's leg, I try smiling past the fear that this may not work at all. It's happened before, though rare. I've read about it. Watched the videos. The thought of our son being one of the few who won't be able to hear...

It breaks my heart.

"Milo?" Instantly, Milo drops the toy and looks up at me. His blue eyes are wide, causing my heart to hammer so hard it physically hurts. "Oh, my God. Hi, baby boy! Can you hear Mommy?" Milo's little lips part in awe as he stares unblinkingly at me.

Ollie says, "Hi, buddy." Milo's eyes turn to his Daddy in a quick bolt of his head, where a big smile spreads across his face.

Tears leak down my cheeks as I hold him against me tightly. "I can't believe this is happening." Trying to calm down, I wipe at my tears and sniff back the oncoming ones. "We're so proud of you, sweetie. Look at you!"

His little laugh surprises him, his body wiggling and hand reaching for his ear. He tugs on the lobe, seemingly in awe over what's happening.

Woodshed taps his knuckles against the edge of his desk. "Milo, look over here." His knuckles wrap louder on the wood, causing Milo to turn and stare at the older man. "Good boy. I'm going to turn it up a little bit and run a few sound tests and see how he reacts. Okay?"

Milo begins making noises, his bottom squirming on my lap as I kiss the back of his head over and over.

Woodshed starts playing a soft alarm sound, the beeping increasing as the seconds drag by. Milo cries out and claps his hands, pointing at the doctor.

"Good job," I praise, not bothering to stop the tears from escaping my eyes. My chest swells so rapidly as I watch Milo react to the other sounds Woodshed throws at him.

Bells.

Whistles.

Laughter.

Milo hears it all.

He. Hears. It. All.

Struggling to swallow past the lump of hardened emotion in the back of my throat, I rock him in my arms while Ollie leans into me. He presses a long kiss against the top of my head, his own cheeks damp with tears.

"Keep talking to him, parents," Woodshed directs, giving me an encouraging smile.

"I love you, Milo. So much."

"So much," Ollie confirms, both of us holding onto him and absorbing his warmth.

Woodshed grabs a plastic toy and jiggles it, letting the beads inside create a new noise for Milo to listen to. When we hear his light laughter, everything inside me bursts.

With joy.

With hope.

With love.

The appointment lasts another hour as we go through the expectations. It'll take time for him to get used to all the sounds, and he'll need plenty of hearing and speech therapy as he gets older to adjust. Since he'll need new ear molds, we're expected to go in for fittings once a month to ensure he'll be able to continue using the aid as his ears grow.

"It's going to be overwhelming for everyone," Woodshed states, giving us a serious expression. "However, you have just given this child something beautiful. You should all be proud of what has been accomplished. Take it a day at a time and don't be afraid to reach out."

"Can I..." I press my lips together. "Will he be able to speak normally? I mean, I know sometimes there's a bit of a speech impediment with the hearing impaired."

"Speech therapy will be able to help," he answers, standing up and flattening his white lab jacket. "There will always be a slight difference in the way he talks though. Are you still planning on teaching him sign language?"

We both nod.

His smile is praising. "Good. It's a useful skill to have. When it comes to schooling, there are plenty of options. There schools for the deaf around, or typical public and private institutions. I'm not saying one is better than the other. As far as I'm concerned, Milo is as normal a kid as the next. However, deaf education can help build skills that kids without impairments already have. In fact, some patients have enrolled their children in schools for the deaf for the first few years to heighten their speech abilities before switching them to public education settings."

Ollie is the one who asks, "But it's not necessary, is it?

We'd like Milo to be raised how we were. I'd hate to think we're isolating him because of his condition."

Woodshed shakes his head, putting one hand in his lab jacket pocket. "It's certainly not required. The only thing I would highly encourage is the hearing therapy. It'll be beneficial to Milo adjusting to hearing after this long of not. Speech therapy too, to prepare him for any type of education you two decide."

We nod along in understanding, knowing we have a lot of decisions to make. But each one we choose will be worth what's been given to Milo. And for that, I'll always be thankful.

In a tiny voice, I ask, "Can I give you a hug, Dr. Woodshed?"

His eyes soften. "Of course."

Passing Milo off to Ollie, I stand and walk over to the man who has changed our lives—changed our son's life. I'll be grateful for him for as long as I live.

"Thank you." I wrap my arms around him and squeeze. He reminds me of Robert James, professional and kind. Someone who loves and is proud of what he does.

"You are more than welcome, Charlie." His large hand pats my back before pulling away, smiling down at me. "And congratulations on baby number two."

I blush. "Thank you. Um..." I wet my bottom lip and shift from one foot to another. "I know you probably wouldn't know, but what is the likelihood that..."

He knows what I'm asking before I can even gather

the courage to speak the words. "I wouldn't focus on what your baby will go through. It all depends on how the genes line up. Some siblings have the same condition, others don't. We can't be sure."

Not knowing what to say, I just smile.

Ollie stands up and shakes his hand. "I can't seem to put to words how much this means to us. Just … thank you. For everything you do for families that need this."

Woodshed clasps his hand. "It's truly my pleasure. Being able to give people a chance to hear is one of the best feelings. And I don't doubt for a second that your family is going to conquer any obstacle along the way."

Milo makes noises, coos, and giggles over every sound. We all laugh, watching him completely awestruck over such a magical feeling. It's amazing what we take for granted daily that others don't have.

When we say goodbye after making an appointment for next month, I settle into the backseat next to Milo. Ollie gets in the front and starts the car, bathing the space in classical music that Milo claps over.

"You like that?" I laugh, tickling his stomach. He giggles and grabs his toes, looking up at me with such a brightness in his eyes I can't help but grin from ear to ear. "You take after Mommy, huh? Are you going to learn how to play the piano?"

He has no idea what I'm saying, but it doesn't stop him from seeming happy over it. We stay like that for about twenty minutes, listening to various songs on the radio before we hit traffic from a construction zone on the highway.

When the high-pitched noise of machinery breaking apart pavement on the left lane grows nearer as we creep along, Milo's eyes glaze with tears. His hands go to his ears and pulls as he belts out a cry that only makes him bawl harder.

"Ollie," I panic, not knowing what to do.

"We're almost out," he assures, speeding up a little to get past the construction.

"We need to get off the highway."

His eyes meet mine in the rearview. "I'd need to take the next exit and that would bring us the long way around. Are you—"

"Please?" I soothe Milo by rubbing his belly and humming to him. "There's more work further ahead. It's too much for him right now."

Ollie nods and moves to merge onto the exit, bringing us down the ramp. When it's safe, he pulls over and parks the car. Turning around, he studies Milo, and then me.

"You okay?"

I don't realize that I'm also crying as I try calming Milo. Managing to nod, I force myself to inhale and flood my lungs with much-needed oxygen. "I'm sorry. Woodshed said it'd be overwhelming, but I didn't realize how much. Milo is going to need so much therapy to get used to these sounds, Ollie. That's a lot of money. And the speech therapy seems like a necessary evil to get him used to talking—"

"We'll be okay. Charlie, breathe." He reaches for my knee and squeezes. "We have the money in my trust fund. I already moved some aside for his schooling, no matter where he goes."

I hiccup. "Do you think he should go to a special school? He needs the extra help, and we can't give him any. We can teach him sign language but that's it."

He shakes his head. "We'll teach him a lot of things, baby. How to be kind. How to work for what you want. How to never get up. When we get home, we'll think about our options. We need to take this one step at a time that way we aren't stressing out about every detail."

He's right. Counting in my head to simmer down, I dry my cheeks and look back at Milo. His eyes are still glazed, but the tears on his cheeks have dried up. I lean down and pepper kisses across his forehead.

"That was scary, huh?"

He coos.

"You're okay, sweetie."

He manages to smile, and that's when I know it's true. Because Milo Brahm James is just like his parents. Strong. Resilient. Nothing that comes his way will stop him.

As a family, we'll get through anything.

EPILOGUE

Six Years Later
Ollie

Two pairs of feet pad toward the kitchen as I finish zipping up the second lunch box and set it by my car keys.

"We're going to be late," I call, just as my little brunette walks into the kitchen with her thumb in her mouth and her brother's hand holding her other.

Aria takes after me in just about all departments— dark hair, dark eyes, and fair complexion. She was born without any complications, passing all the newborn tests the hospital did on her. Charlie didn't experience the same difficulties following the birth, and Milo genuinely seemed excited to be a big brother.

I can tell it's hard on him though. He loves his little sister and protects her just as I did with River when she was adopted. But the way he watches her interact, hears her talk, brings a dull to his eyes as a reminder they're different in more than just looks.

"You okay, Ari?"

She pops her finger out of her mouth. "I don't wanna go to school today."

I kneel to her level. "Why not?"

It's Milo who says, "The other kids pick on her." I notice how he tightens his hold.

My frown matches the one on Aria's face. I reach out and pulls her into me, giving her a tight hug. "What are they saying, sweetheart?"

When she pulls back, her eyes are pointed toward the ground. I know it must be rough if she doesn't make eye contact. Both kids tend to avoid looking at us when they're uncomfortable. Like when Milo wrote all over the walls in permanent marker two years ago and tried pretending like it'd always been there.

"It's about me," Milo murmurs.

My eyes widen. "What?"

Milo crosses his arms over his chest and kicks at the floor with the tip of his little beige work boot. "They know I don't go there because I'm deaf. When we went to her open house, they heard me talk. How I ... don't sound right."

Nostrils flaring, I reach out for him. "You don't sound any different than them, Milo. Come on, buddy. I know it's been hard, but—"

"Can I go to school there?"

I blink. Charlie and I have discussed letting him transfer once he finished the year off at Callie's School for the Deaf, that way him and Aria can be in the same elementary school. "Do you want that? Your mother and I discussed it, but we thought you liked your school."

His lips tip downward. "I do."

"If there are problems—"

"Dad," he cuts me off. "I want to be where Aria is. It isn't fair that she's being picked on because of me. Just because I'm different."

Swallowing past the anger bubbling over a bunch of asshole kids, I give him a terse nod and force myself to calm down. "Tell you what. When we're all home tonight, we'll go over things with Mom. Sound like a deal?"

Aria sticks her thumb in her mouth, then moves it to ask, "Why am I not death?"

"Deaf," I correct, emphasizing the *f*. Brushing hair behind her ear, I smile at her. "We talked about this, Ari. You were born with the ability to hear."

She almost looks disappointed that she's not like her brother, and it makes me want to chuckle. Instead, I kiss her cheek and then stand up. Rubbing Milo's head, I back up and notice the lack of backpacks near them.

"Backpacks. Now."

Milo sighs and walks into the entryway to grab both of their bags. Just as I'm grabbing them a couple Pop Tarts to take with us, I notice Aria's bright purple bag moving in the slightest way. The sound coming from it has me quickly reaching for it despite her pleas.

Our black and white cat, appropriately named Oreo, jumps out and bolts into the other room. My eyes go to

Aria, who's once more looking down at the hardwood floor.

"We talked about this," I remind her.

"But it's show and tell..."

Milo takes her hand. "Oreo doesn't like people, remember? Mom says she's like that lady from the grocery store who looks like she has something shoved up her—"

I clap loudly. "Okay. Here's some breakfast. Don't tell your Mom I gave them to you so early. She's under a lot of stress trying to finalize the deal for her new location."

About six months after Aria was born, Charlie mentioned wanting to expand her business because more people were getting in touch with her about her music therapy lessons. We looked at different buildings in town but couldn't find one that would work for one reason or another. She decided not to worry about it until this year when I offered the idea of building a guest house on our property that she could run her business from. Her client numbers have climbed enough where it's getting harder to continue running it from the spare room.

As of two weeks ago, the structure itself was completed and given the proper okay to do what she needed to it. Now she's in the final stages of setting everything up and making sure everything is perfect. I even surprised her with business cards so she can start distributing them.

"Mommy?" Aria says.

I reach for her hand. "She had to meet someone early this morning, but she'll be here when you two get back."

She nods and shoves her thumb back into her mouth, a habit we're struggling to get her to break. Milo is quiet as we all load into the car. It's become routine to drop him off first and then bring Aria in with me since we're both at the same district. It'll be easier once Milo is too, that way we won't be as rushed in the morning.

When I pull up in the drop off section, I turn to face Milo. Giving him a big smile, I sign, *I love you* like I always do before he gets out.

He hesitates, looking out the window like he's embarrassed over someone seeing him sign it back. When he sees only a few teachers waiting for last-minute students to be dropped off, he signs it and says it back since Aria only knows part of the alphabet so far.

I watch Milo and one of the teacher's aides sign each other in greeting before entering the school side by side. He looks back and waves, getting a frantic wave back from his sister.

Shaking my head and stifling a laugh, I pull away and head back toward the interstate to get us where we need to be before the first bell rings. Usually we're not this behind, but both kids were dragging their feet this morning.

After a few minutes of nothing but the radio going, Aria says, "Can we get a puppy?"

What the fuck?

Unlike the argument I lost with Charlie on the cat we

adopted from the shelter, I'm determined to put my foot down.

"Dogs are a lot of work, Aria."

"Please?"

"Sorry, sweetie."

"Pretty please?"

"Ari." I sigh and recall the similar conversation at the zoo with Charlie. "We're not getting a dog. Please stop asking."

Her silence is both welcoming and surprising but knowing her it's not the last I'll hear of the matter. Especially if she gets her brother in on it. I groan just thinking about it, turning the radio up to drown out the thought.

"A puppy would make you happy."

I just sigh.

EPILOGUE TWO

One Year Later
Charlie

Milo won't let me hold his hand when we walk toward the Liberty Elementary entrance, which I try not to take to heart. He's seven now, growing up. I doubt he wants to be seen at his new school holding his mother's hand. I wouldn't have wanted that either.

Even though he knows where he's going, I can't help but double check. "Do you remember your teacher's name and classroom?"

His groan is loud as we stop outside the Main Office. "Yes, Mom. You and Dad asked me that like four times already."

"We just want to be sure."

He's gotten taller over the past year, he's already up to my chest. Something tells me he'll easily get to Ollie's six-four height. I just hope Aria doesn't sprout as quickly as Milo, or we'll be going through clothes again like crazy.

I smooth out his shirt. "I have to sign some last-minute paperwork and then I'll be out of your hair. You know you can reach me anytime if you need something, right? If there are any problems—"

"Mom."

I take a deep breath. "Sorry. I love you."

He doesn't sign it, making my lips twitch a little. I know he worries about what other kids will say about him using that to communicate. He's also mentioned to Ollie that he doesn't want the other kids to laugh at his implants. "Love you too, Mom. I'll be okay."

Hearing him say that makes the waterworks want to flood my face, but I force them back, so I don't embarrass him. We've been telling him that for so long, it's no surprise he says it so easily. What's great is that he believes it because he knows he's ready for this.

He gives me a cautious glance. "Oh, and I think Doug puked in my room this morning."

My lips part. "You're just telling me this now? Why didn't you clean it up?"

"It's Aria's dog!"

I sigh, scrubbing my hands down my face. The last thing I expected was Ollie to bring up getting a dog when he seemed reluctant about getting Oreo. When I realized it was what Aria wanted, it all clicked into place.

My husband is a sucker.

"Fine. I'll look when I get back."

When we walk into the Main Office, I tell the secretary it's Milo's first day. From the corner of my eye, I notice a little girl sitting off to the side, swinging her legs back and forth in a bright blue chair. She stares at the floor, playing with her fingers, while a woman who looks slightly familiar speaks in low tones with the other secretary.

She must notice me watching, because she looks over and blinks. Her head tilts and I wonder if we've seen each other before. Her hair is red, natural by the looks of it, but I don't put the pieces together right away.

"Sorry," I apologize. "Do we know each other? You just look—"

"Really familiar," she finishes, walking over and sticking out her hand. "I'm Piper."

Piper...?

My eyes widen. "Like Piper from the hospital? My husband Oliver and I were there with Milo when he was little. I think we met in the waiting room. I'm Charlie."

Surprise flickers across her face. She gestures behind her to the little girl. Milo notices and looks around the woman's body to get a better look. "That's right. Ainsley and I were there with her father Daniel. Wow. And this is Milo? You guys go here now?"

Milo walks over to the little girl, causing her to look up. "It's his first day. His little sister has attended since pre-k, but he attended a different institution."

Piper notices Milo talking to the little girl, and her face pales a little. "Ainsley doesn't talk. I should—" She stops talking when she sees Milo begin signing to her, which makes Ainsley's eyes brighten as she quickly responds with her hands.

My heart warms at the sight of them communicating, something he worried himself sick about since we agreed to transfer him.

"She never..." Piper clears her throat. "I don't think

anyone outside my family knows sign language. Nobody speaks to her that way."

I'm not sure what makes me do it, but I reach out and squeeze her hand. She smiles at me gratefully. "We taught Milo after he got the implants that way he had a different way to communicate if talking made him too uncomfortable. He can do both, but we wanted the option there."

Piper's smile is filled with emotion. "I know Ainsley will appreciate it. Sometimes I worry about her. It's hard making friends when she's...."

I don't ask what her condition is. I vaguely remember hearing her talk for a microsecond in the surgical waiting room. Whatever happened since is none of my business.

But I know her pain well. I've worried the same about Milo but can easily see neither of us should focus on that concern. I let go of her hand when the secretary passes me a few forms to read over and sign.

"How old is he?" she asks.

"Seven."

Her eyes peek back at them. "Ainsley can show him where to go if you'd like. She's been here her whole life."

I'm about to tell her that Milo is set on finding it himself when he walks over and tugs on the hem of my shirt. "Can Ainsley take me to the classroom?"

"Of course." I smile at Piper, who looks awestruck as Ainsley walks over and signs something to her rapidly. I try not to eavesdrop, so I fix Milo's hair and then squeeze his shoulders. "I hope you have a great first day."

He hesitates, then signs, *I will. Thank you.*

Piper and I watch them leave the office, still signing back and forth. When they're out of view, I lean against the counter and let out a heavy sigh.

"They grow up fast, huh?" she asks.

"Too fast," I murmur.

"Hey." She pauses. "It'd be nice to have more friends. If you ever need anything..."

I take advantage of the opportunity and pull out a business card Ollie had made for me that has my cell listed. "Same goes for you. My cell and email are both listed. Who knows? Maybe our kids will become good friends."

I can tell by the way her green eyes lighten that she wants the same thing. It's strange to me how so many years of battles and hardships can somehow feel like nothing when opportunities like this present themselves.

Milo and Aria are at the same school.

I have a business I'm proud of.

Ollie loves his job.

And we're happy.

Honest to God happy.

About the Author

B. Celeste's obsession with all things forbidden and taboo enabled her to pave a path into a new world of raw, real, emotional romance.

Her debut novel is The Truth about Heartbreak.

Made in the USA
Monee, IL
05 August 2024

63251364R00076